ISOLATE

TO

ELEVATE

Sometimes God isolates us to elevate us.

CELEATH TURNER

To buy in bulk email: sales@themangogirl.com

Editing, book cover design and interior formatting by: Mango Girl Group Ltd Publishing.

Special thanks to Master Book Coach: Dr Ava Eagle Brown.

Mango Girl Group Ltd. Publishing

DEDICATION

This book is dedicated to those who endured isolation
in the Corona Virus, take it as God trying to
communicate with you individually.

Table of Contents

Quotes and references:

Scriptures quotations are from:

The Holy Bible, New King James (KJV)

Preface

During the third week of the coronavirus lockdown, when I realised that the world was not going to open for a while, it suddenly dawned on me that God was angry with the world. Also, the coronavirus may have been man-made according to the speculations. I know that God had control over everything. Then I realised as I went deeper in thought, it dawned on me that God has isolated the world in order that he could be elevated but more so, I took it on a deeper level and realised that he isolates us sometimes to take us to another level. For example, I'm not boasting or anything like that but before the coronavirus had started I was busy with life, being a mom, being active with the church and I have always had this desire to write a book but I was not able to properly do it until I was isolated.

You see isolation gives you time. It gives you that time to be by yourself, to be within your thoughts and that time to be deeper within yourself and ultimately to dig deeper into the word of God. As a matter of fact, a number of people have become fearful and despite their fear, good or bad, they have been isolated so that they can be pushed towards to bible, pushed towards the scripture, pushed towards re-establishing themselves with God. I have seen many and I have heard of many people who because of this coronavirus decided to turn their life around and getting closer to Christ because of the isolation.

I can think of many times in the bible when isolation took place. For example, I am going to mention within the book that Jesus went up on the Mount of Olive and he isolated himself. Not because he did not love his disciples, not because they were not important, but because he needed to be one on one. He needed stillness. I want you to be calm and be still, close your eyes; close out everything. Isolate yourself in that moment from everybody around you and be in stillness. I want you to write down everything you hear and everything you see.

God has inspired me to write this book because I believe that God wants his children to know that in order for them to elevate in him from one level or another, they must first go through a period of being isolated so that they do not become distracted by the things in the world but rather to focus of him. God gave me this subject because within the body of Christ more and more saints are losing focus on what needs to be done, and the thing they should be focused on. They become so complacent. They believe that just because they are already in a certain position that they do not need to be elevated to a higher one, which God had called and chosen for them to be in.

As we know during our isolation period, we tend to feel like we are alone, but we have to remember that God said that he will never leave you nor forsake you so as we are going through our trials and tribulations, God is there throughout. What this book does is elaborate on what the bible teaches us about Isolation, what we face when we are in our season of Isolation, and why we need to be isolated to get elevated by God.

The purpose of this book is to help those who are in their state of isolation to understand why God has put them in that season or for those who have not as yet been in their season of isolation to know what to expect when they enter into that season of isolation. By reading this book you as reader will learn how to get through your season of isolation and to be expecting your elevation.

During our period of isolation, we must hold onto our faith so that we can get through our isolation season and reach our elevation period. When you have entered your season of isolation you must ensure that you continue to fast, pray, reading the bible and worshipping God. You must ensure that your heart, mind, and soul is focused on him because you want to make sure that you are showing God you want to be elevated through him.

"This is the day which the Lord hath made; we will rejoice and be glad in it" (Psalm 118:24).

In your period of isolation, you will not get:

- ✓ Depressed

- ✓ Oppressed

- ✓ Supressed

- ✓ Stressed

Remember Job was in isolation during his period of testing. Remember, he had to struggle alone through one thing after another, which tested his faith but despite it all, Job did not give up but rather he continued and progressed through the trial God had put into place for him. By doing so, he moved closer to God. Yes, we know that he may have been feeling alone because his friends and his wife turned against him during his isolation period.

Often God allows us to go into our isolation period so that when we come out of it, we come out much stronger, anointed, powerful, empowered, equipped, rooted, and grounded within Christ.

When you are feeling down, rejected, and hurt during your isolation period, speak into your situation, and say nothing just happened. During your isolation period, you may feel like everyone has walked away from you but when people can walk away from you let them walk because you know that you cannot get elevated if they are still in the picture. Some of these people come to discourage, distract, and destroy the plan and purpose that God has destined for your life and where he wants to place you in ministry.

Saints of God, often we feel like we are all alone and God is nowhere to be seen or found.

"And we know that all things work together for good to them that love God, to them who are the called according to his purpose" (Romans 8:28).

I want to leave you all today with a song:

Though the battle may be hot

And the conflict slow

Though rugged the road

As you travel along

Hold on a little longer

Take Jesus at His word

He will carry you through, right through

To the promise land.

You see that is what isolation does, it literally elevates you and you do not have to be physically moved away from people. You can learn to isolate in your mind. You can shut out the world and go to an elevated place in your mind. So, come with me on this journey as I show you what isolation means to me. I hope at the end of reading this book that you to will be elevated, whether in your mind, your thoughts, or your personal relationship with God.

Thank you very much.

Chapter 1

Isolation

The best example of isolation in my view is when Christ went to Mount Olive. He showed us that even though he loved the people he just fed and even more so his disciples, he needed that space and time to be free to think and connect with his father.

We all know the bible scripture when Jesus went up on Mount Olive, he wanted to separate himself from his disciples. He literally and physically extracted himself because he needed to be isolated. To communicate with his father.

Now a few of us might be wondering why but the bible says that he needed not to communicate until further notice (Matthew 14:23). When Jonah was in the whale's belly, he was isolated. There are several places in the bible where people were separated, removed from everything that was around them and the first example of that was Jesus Christ himself on the mountain.

"And when he had sent the multitudes away, he went up into a mountain apart to pray and when the evening was come, he was there alone" (Matthew 14:23).

The bible is teaching us that there are sometimes in our life where we need to be isolated or in a place of isolation. Let us talk about what happened to God when he went up on Mount Olive. When we Look into the results of it, Jesus when he went on the mountain, he needed to take himself away from his disciples or any form of person or things that would distract him from fulfilling his father's work or plan and so that he could draw closer to God. Another example of being isolated to fulfil Gods work was a man named Jonah. Jonah was a prophet in the land of Israel whom God wanted to use to bring forth a message to the people of Nineveh.

"Now the word of the Lord came unto Jonah the son of Amittai, saying, Arise, go to Nineveh, that great city, and cry against it; for their wickedness is come up before me. But Jonah rose up to flee unto Tarshish from the presence of the Lord, and went down to Joppa; and he found a ship going to Tarshish: so, he paid the fare thereof, and went down into it, to go with them unto Tarshish from the presence of the Lord" (Jonah 1:1-3).

When God told Jonah to warn the people of Nineveh to repent, the prophet turned the other direction and fled, he had run away from his commitment, not understanding that his actions would suffer consequences. What God had then done was send a whale to swallow Jonah up for his will to be fulfilled and his message to be delivered to the sinful people of Nineveh.

When Jonah came out of the whale's belly what happened? He went to Nineveh and Nineveh was saved, because of Jonah being swallowed up in the whale's belly and having been forced to be isolated from the world for 3 days and 3 nights. God wanted to remove him from his noisy surroundings because he had become immune to the voice of God and because of his wanting to be disobedient.

There are too many voices that Jonah was listening too and the only voice he needed to listen to was God. It is the same way that sometimes in our life God must isolate us for us to hear from him. Now, you may be wondering, or probably some of you may already know the prudency of this message or the topic of this book. All of us have gone through a period of isolation during the Coronavirus pandemic (COVID-19), a word we will never forget.

Now, for a lot of us, during this isolation period, we would have gotten better, spent time with the family, or reflected on ourselves during the time away from the world and others may have been fearful of it as they were worrying that God was coming and it being the end of the world. Whatever your ideology is on why we went through that isolation it is irrelevant. What I know is that sometimes God must separate you, isolate you, remove you, extract you to elevate you.

When we are in isolation this will give us time to build and create ourselves without having any form of distraction as we can have a clear mind to think about what is the next thing we want to achieve in our life. When we are going through this process, we will gain self-acceptance and independence. It may be hard while you are going through it, but it will be worth it in the end. I want to let you all know that we cannot be beneficial to anyone in any situation until we become whole within ourselves. Let me give you an example as we have all been a customer at some point in our lives. We are more likely to purchase as product (ourselves), we are more than likely to make the sale (perform), the challenges we face with isolation. It is not that we do not want to be alone, but it is the fact that we are concerned about how others will feel about our absence.

Now, think about when is baby is born, when a man, and woman come together they make love, they produce a child. When the baby is in the womb, if you notice that God in his infinite wisdom did not leave the baby on the outside because the God I know could have instantaneously, literally matured the baby to be walking around in no time. Instead, he understood that the baby needed certain nurturing, the baby needed to develop. So, he left the baby in the mother's womb, attached to the umbilical cord, which links the child to the mother, feeding it for nine months. Now, as you guys know, the baby had to go through a birthing season and its own season of isolation. There was a reason why the child stayed in the belly for nine months. God isolated the infant so not even their own parents could reach them. And so, let us talk about what happens during the infant's isolation.

If you ever been pregnant, or if you have never experienced pregnancy, I would like to share the development of giving birth to a baby boy or girl. You should know that at birth and between 6-8 weeks, a baby's head circumference will be measured to check the size and growth of the brain. The baby's weight is also measured. These measurements provide information on how well the baby is growing. Usually, healthy new-born's double their birth weight by 4-5 months and triple it by 1 year.

During physical development of an infant, the baby learns how to control their movements in their body first, then their arms and legs. They also develop social and emotional skills during this time. This is the development of a child's identity and self-image. The development of relationships and feelings about him or herself and learning the skills to live in society with other people.

In addition, a baby intellectually develops by means of gaining learning skills that include such things as understanding, memory, and concentration. They learn communication and speech development, which they need to communicate with friends, family, and all others.

Have you ever wondered why God has allowed a new-born baby to grow up and develop these skills throughout their lifetime? The reason behind God doing so is to show us that each and every individual has a purpose and to get to the level he wants you to reach, you need to be able to function. You need to be able to use your physical, social, emotional, and intellectual skills that will help you to elevate in him in a different level spiritually. As the scripture says in Isaiah 28:10, "For precept must be upon precept, precept upon precept; line upon line, line upon line; here a little, and there a little."

"For I know the thoughts that I think toward you, saith the Lord, thoughts of peace, and not of evil, to give you an expected end" (Jeremiah 29:11).

These people who have read this scripture are people who have gone through obstacles for what you already have. You need a promise for what you do not have, for what you do not see. This promise, in Jeremiah 29, is profound because God says, I know the thoughts that I think towards you. Why is that such a comfort towards us? It is a comfort to us because there are days in our lives when all hell is breaking loose and we wonder where God is. There are also two voices that talk both at the same time and when trouble comes, and storms arise, and oppositions begin to oppress, one voice always speaks up and says, "Where is your God? I thought you had so much faith. I thought you were such a Christian and a believer."

Look at your situation right now. This promise comes from God saying you may be going through a tough time of isolation right now but do not attribute it to my thoughts for I know the thoughts I have towards you are thoughts of peace and not evil to give you an expected end. The things that I am planning. The things that I have in-store for you, the things that I have been up all night preparing for you, are thoughts of peace and not evil. Then he says that you may have life and have an expected end and that when everything is said and done things will turn out alright. He was not thinking any evil against me. Thoughts of peace and not evil. God said he will listen unto you and harken unto you. So, call upon God during your isolation and he will listen to you, answer your prayers, and bring you out and when everything ends and how it turns out it will be alright. Shout from the top of your voice in your isolation that it will turn out alright.

There is time that we as Christians forget about the end, and we forget the middle. God did not say that you will have an expected middle or an expected beginning, but he said you will have an expected end. That is why we need faith for the end, for as Hebrews 11:1 says, "Now faith is the substance of things hoped for, the evidence of things not seen." That is why we need faith because through faith we embrace the expected end of elevation.

There may be turbulence in the flight of isolation, but I will land my plane to elevation. You may have to fasten your seatbelts; you may not be comfortable but when everything is said and done, I am going to end this flight.

I live through the isolation then I have had a good experience leading up to my elevation. It might have gotten rough and tough, you may have to buckle up unexpectedly, you might not have watched the movie properly or you may have not been able to fellowship with others at church. It may not have been what you have predicted it to be. We might have been delayed somewhere or we might have had to land somewhere and fly back to where you were trying to go. You might be late arriving at your destination, hungry when you get there or even exhausted when you, but I am alive to tell the story in my view because it was a good experience in isolation. I heard some things, I have matured in some ways, I have gone through some things. I have found out that turbulence does not mean destruction. I am such an experienced flyer now that when I fly with people that are not used to flying and I see them getting nervous in their time of isolation, I look over at them and smile because I have been through it already.

I have been through flights that cannot shake me with a little humps and bumps and a little turbulence. One of the benefits of elevating is you have seen enough turbulence and seen enough storms, and because of that you know when to hold it and when to fold it. You know when to walk away from situations or you when to just be still. You may also know how to encourage yourself and say, this too shall pass.

You need to understand that in the world that we live in, that much of what we face is not as perplexing as how we feel about what we face. It is not what you go through, it is how you feel about what you go through. It is your emotional reaction to what you go through. It is the agony you go through internally about it that makes it as severe as it is. Other people may have gone through a time of isolation like you and it is a smooth sailing because they do not have turbulence or inner turmoil, which comes from expectation. When things do not go as they are expected to and we experience stress, it is because we have a need to be in control of everything. We get frustrated because it is not going according to how we expected it to go.

Sometimes during isolation, you feel stressed out, and it seems like if someone were to tap you on the shoulder, you would break into a million little pieces! Everything seems out of place, church, house, relationships, jobs, or the direction you are heading. You feel as if you are at your breaking point and are wanting to scream all the time. That is where you keep on repeating Lord, I need you to show up for me now because I cannot take the pressure anymore. I cannot take anymore! You feel like crying at random times of the day. You feel like God is tugging on you to pray more for you to break through and break free of all that you are facing.

You have prayed and cried, prayed, and cried some more. Lord, what should I do concerning my time in isolation? How can I get over this situation? How do I handle my area of gifting when I do not even fully understand that which you have placed upon me? Lord, people seem to be ganging up against me, scheming to destroy my life, my ministry, my destiny, and my purpose. They do not even recognise who I am or the heavy weight of the mandate that you have laid upon me and that I am going through a rough season of isolation where I am being tested and tempted all the time in every area, measure, and method.

I want to let you know that God is working. Saint, do not get it twisted! You are in the last few weeks, days, and hours of your spiritual pregnancy and still in pain from your isolation season. It is time to rejoice! To holler and shout. The labour pains are becoming more frequent, my God from Zion, but it is because you are truly pregnant with something in the spirit! Throughout, you have heard many people speak about being "pregnant", but you have never experienced it. Oh dear, you are beginning to get uncomfortable. Your tummy has become quite heavy, your feet are swollen, and you can hardly walk or even eat. You cannot even sit or lay down in a comfortable position. Pain is rocking from all directions over your body and you are ready to deliver this baby! Come on now Jesus. This is a time of excitement and anticipation! It is a time of preparation for the arrival of the "baby"! More prayer is required, more sensitivity to the Holy Spirit.

When you are pregnant and have been in isolation, you must recognise that there is a process to birthing the gift. When a woman is pregnant, she has no control over the amount of weight that she will gain or the morning sickness she will suffer, the mood changes, or appetite the baby inside of her controls all of that. Just like in the spirit, we have no control. We yield everything unto our Lord and Saviour Jesus Christ. His will be done. Do not get distracted in this season. Get in position and get ready to PUSH!!!! Thank God for the gift.

Push for that elevation, PUSH! That is why your church members seem to be against you. That is why your own family members will not help you. You are pregnant, and you are glowing in the Spirit! Saints of God, rejoice in the fact that the pressure is there. All the weight, pressure, and unusual experiences are all a part of being pregnant within your level of elevation. But here is what we know. The baby MUST come out, and when it does, we will see that all the preparation was worth it.

Chapter 2

Baby Christians

Within the body of Christ, we can identify some Christians as baby Christians. Now, when we are talking about baby Christians, I do not mean literally babies that are Christians. What I am saying to you today, is that there are people who in the body of Christ, call themselves Christians, who are not fully matured Christians yet. Dealing with people who seemingly cannot grow up is difficult. They can drag you down and often act like leeches that suck the life and joy out of you. Just as people can be spoiled in the natural, there are also those who are spoiled in the spiritual. These are the people who have remained spiritual babies for far too long.

1 Peter 2:2 reminds us that we all start out as babies, **"Like new-born infants, long for the pure spiritual milk, that by it you may grow up into salvation." But even as we start as spiritual infants, the goal is for us to "grow up in salvation."**

Spiritual immaturity can bring about problems not just to the person but to the people around that person. Here are six signs of spiritual stagnation that should convince us that it's time to grow up spiritually and if we do not grow spiritually, then we will not be able to elevate in God, in the different dimension and realm in God. This is simply because:

You Do Not Read the Word of God

The primary way to grow is to be fed. When we are not fed physically, we then do not grow physically. The same is true for our spirits. When was the last time you "fed" on God's Word? If it does not happen regularly, it is not happening enough.

You are Not Getting Involved in Ministry

Spiritual maturity is marked by a capacity to be on the serving end instead of being the one always served. If you are consuming spiritually, it is dangerous because it gets us lazy and immature. As Proverbs 11:25 tells us, "Whoever brings blessing will be enriched, and one who waters will himself be watered."

There Is Little Generosity on Your Part

Aside from being generous with our service that we give unto others, we can also be generous with our time and resources that we have. When we refuse to be generous, this just shows the level of stagnation we are in. When we truly grow in Christ, we will experience an outflow of grace that we will want to be channels to others.

You Do Not Like Correction

Rebuke and correction may not be nice, but it is our way of becoming disciplined in the spirit. When we refuse discipline, just as children who are deprived of it, we tend to stop growing or to grow a lot slower than we should, just like a plant that is not being watered or fed to grow.

Your Talk Rarely Turns into Action

Being all talk and no action, is also a sign of spiritual immaturity. God calls us to live a life of faith, and faith when genuine will always result in good works. James 2:17 tells us, "Thus also faith by itself, if it does not have works, is dead."

You Cannot Find It in Yourself to Share Your Faith

Do you share your faith with others? Spoiled children are in no position to share because they do not feel like they have anything to share. Spiritually spoiled people act the same way as well. When we truly grow in Christ, we will be compelled to preach, teach, exalt, encourage, and live the gospel for others to see. For the bible says in Matthew 5:16, "Let your light so shine before men, that they may see your good works, and glorify your Father which is in heaven"

Do you see what isolation does? You are nourished, you are prepared, you have been fed, watered, grounded, and rooted. You see isolation is not meant to kill you but to build you and a lot of us get it wrong by thinking that isolation means that God has forgotten about you. I am sure that there are a few you in the COVID-19 period that were angry at God, saying God, where are you? I have paid my tithes, I have paid my offerings, I have worshipped you, I have been a good girl or boy, and you had left me to die. But let me ask a question right now, how many have come out of COVID-19 stronger, more resilient, more focused on what really matters, your previous lifestyle of materialism having been conquered.

Isolation is widespread in today's culture and society. It is an epidemic throughout every part of the world and in the churches. Everyone has experienced this unpleasant feeling of isolation at one point or another within their lives. Think back to that time on the fairground when all the children of different age and gender were playing with friends and you were sitting on the sidewalk. Remember wanting to join in with them but being either too shy or fearful to approach them or perhaps they never made an attempt to approach you and invite you to play with them? Or maybe you had an uncomfortable experience in high school when you were left out on many occasions because nobody saw you as approachable enough. Perhaps you were even labelled by other peers as awkward, weird, or different from the rest. It could have been that they may have been jealous of you for unknown reasons. You may have been generally nervous growing up where you could not communicate well to most people or keep a conversation going for exceptionally long. You grew up in a very isolated environment, which made it extremely hard and difficult for you to connect and socialise with others and engage in social activities. As a result, you may have tried to keep yourself apart to avoid judgment, problems, and ridicule from others. In college, you might have met some wonderful people who helped you realise the depths of God's love and saving grace that drew you to him.

Here is an exercise that will help. Take a pen out and a piece of paper and write down what have you learned from being in isolation. I have learned that family and the people you love are most important. We have learned to do with what we have.

How many of you went to buy clothes in COVID-19?

How many of you kept on buying things when you did not need them?

Before the pandemic, Christians may have taken for granted their ability to worship God in person at churches. This situation should be a wake-up call to all that discern and resist any deliberate efforts to curb freedom of worship in the future. We should remember the faithful Christians in China who are cut off from even meeting online and understand such isolation as persecution.

In reflecting on our past, we can learn from it. How does the church survive its isolation and finally thrive? We face adversity with faith. We reach out however we can help each other and our neighbours by any means necessary.

You seem, isolation was there to make you realise that half of the things that you were buying and storing up in the fridge and in your closet, were not needed. So, God had to pull back the curtain to let us be reminded of who he was and who he is now and who he will always be.

I think what God is trying to tell us is that we have been too busy with the world, been too busy with our family, too busy trying to chase everything except chasing him.

So, he had to step in like the all mighty and powerful God that he is and say enough is enough. You have forgotten about him and who he is, we were acting like we were God. Think about it. You see, doctors were changing men into women and women into men and they are creating sheep and cloning it here and there and for a moment, the world, the earth, Gods creation, forgot who they were. Sometimes as parents, our children are misbehaving, and they carry on and carry on badly. Growing up in Jamaica, my mother would step in and clear her throat, or catch our eyes and give us that look, and we would just step into line because she was in authority. That is what God does in isolation. He does not clear his throat, he just steps up and clears a situation, just like he did with Jonah so that we can remember who he is.

I am putting this in for your consideration that God may not have created the coronavirus, but he allowed this to happen because he is a God that can do all things. So, he allowed it to happen so that we could recognise whose he is, whose we are but more so for some of us, who are heavenly bound, he had to isolate us to elevate us. Let me ask you a question. How many of you can say that you have gotten closer to God since you were in COVID-19? How many of you forgot who God was during COVID-19 and you are now remembering? You see we should not be in a place where we have forgotten who God is. We had to go through a disastrous thing to remind us. The bible says fix your eyes upon Jesus (Hebrews 12:2). We should have fixed our eyes upon him. So, I think the reason why God must do this is because our eyes were removed. Sometimes, when we are watching tv and are so focused into this movie and somebody comes in with your favourite chicken and you just take you eye of the screen for a split second, the favourite or best part of the movie passes. That is exactly what happens to us with God. We take our eyes off God, we took our eyes off the screen, the screen here represents God and so God must elevate us through isolation.

Ladies and gentlemen let me say something to you. It is no longer a time for us to continue playing around, because COVID-19 was just a warning. It was a simple warning of what God can do. So, the next time he will not separate us to elevate us but instead he will take those who he needs and who are truly his with him to glory.

Often within a person's life, God will set you apart and separate you. He will put you into a place of isolation to bring you forth into another level, realm, and dimension in him regarding the plan he has for your life. For some people, going through this process it can become extremely hard because those who are in your midst may not understand where God is about to take you. When God wants to take you to a certain place, he will ensure that you end up there.

If you have your Bibles, I want you to turn to the book of Proverbs 1. I am teaching a message today entitled isolation. I want to deal with some important things from the Word of God that hopefully will encourage you and those around you to make sure that you are intentional as part of God's community. There is a certain season of our lives where we can be pressed down and weighed down with the pressures of life. Sometimes those pressures make us want to retreat from them.

A man who isolates himself seeks his own desire. He rages against all wise judgment. Is there anybody today besides me who has ever been around a person who has not been around others for too long? Maybe your assessment is like mine where the person has a weirdness about them. People that withdraw themselves from the public, they start getting a little off, they behave differently than the normal expected behaviour. They start saying some things that seem crazy and they start acting in ways that are far off because outside of community the only voice you are hearing is your own. I do not know if you know this or not but for long periods of time if you are only hearing your own voice, it is not a good thing. It is probably a good thing for you to know that you need a time to reflect and think deeply within yourself why God is no longer communicating with you.

Isolated Christians care for themselves and pursue their own interests. (Proverbs 18:1) As believers, we play an integral role in exercising our spiritual gifts, fostering growth and development, keeping each other accountable, praying for one another, teaching and edifying all for the sake of building up the church and glorifying God (1 Corinthians 12, Ephesians 3:8-11, Ephesians 4:12, Acts 2:44-47, James 5:16, Matthew 18:19-20).

For years, you stumbled blindly into the murky waters of sin, which pulled you deeper into laziness, idleness, poor self-control, anger, bitterness, self-pity, a decreased appetite for God's Word, more selfishness, and loneliness that kept getting worse. If you are currently there, run, get out of there before it is too late! There is nothing more terrifying than drowning out the voice of the Holy Spirit with your fleshly desires.

If you feel like you are in a perpetual season of loneliness and isolation, trust me when I tell you that it is only temporary. Loneliness due to isolation is a feeling, and like all feelings they come and go like the fleeting winds. They should never dictate what you know intellectually is true from God's Word. I know circumstances can make it exceedingly difficult to believe, but that should not stop you from living a life of obedience and commitment to God. During loneliness and isolation, we may realize that it is a season filled with an opportunity to grow closer to our Lord and Saviour Jesus Christ. We must ensure that we are not deceived by our human emotions and desires of the heart as well as the lies of the enemy, which is telling us that God is not enough to bring us full satisfaction. May we place our trust in what God says in His Word. If we do this, just think of the many people that would come to know Jesus through our willingness and obedience, not based on how we "feel", but what we "know." When we fail, may we rest in the fact that God will always be with us to the very end (Matthew 28:20).

"For I am convinced that neither death nor life, neither angels nor principalities, neither the present nor the future, nor any powers, neither height nor depth, nor anything else in all creation, will be able to separate us from the love of God that is in Christ Jesus our Lord" (Romans 8:38-39).

"For this reason I bow my knees before the Father, from whom every family in heaven and on earth is named, that according to the riches of his glory he may grant you to be strengthened with power through his Spirit in your inner being, so that Christ may dwell in your hearts through faith—that you, being rooted and grounded in love, may have strength to comprehend with all the saints what is the breadth and length and height and depth, and to know the love of Christ that surpasses knowledge, that you may be filled with all the fullness of God" (Ephesians 3:14-19).

Remember, when a person isolates themselves, they start seeking their own desires and therefore they start raging against all wisdom or plain old common sense. They think it is useless to them.

They will say, *I do not need that advice. I do not need you to tell me what to do I have my own relationship with God. Only god can judge me. I do not need anybody else to say anything to me. I know what I am supposed to do in this situation.*

I want to show you in scripture that I know God is all-sufficient. I know that he is all-knowing, I know that he is omnipresent, I know that he is everything that we need but according to scripture in Genesis 2:18, it says, **"then the Lord God said it is not good for man to be alone." Now, I want to point out here that there is a period after that statement. I will make a helper who is just right for him"** Genesis 2:18.

God makes this statement because Adam is in a blissful relationship with him. God says that it is not good for the man to be alone. He is the one that makes the statement because he understands how important relationships are. Hence why he puts you in isolation. God is okay with you not being enough. He completely understands as it says in Exodus 4:13-16 when Moses pleaded, Lord please send anyone else. Then the Lord became angry with Moses. All right he said, what about your brother Aaron, the Levite. I know he speaks well and look he is on his way to meet you now. He will be delighted to see you. Talk to him and put the words in his mouth. I will be with both of you as you speak, and I will instruct you both in what to do. Aaron will be your spokesman to the people, he will be your mouthpiece and you will stand in the place of God for him.

Telling him what to say but let me remind you of what has culminated here before God goes into this conversation with Moses. There is a bush that is burning that has not burned up. Moses is on the side of a mountain and he sees a bush that is being consumed with fire but would not burn up! Then the bush starts talking to him. That would be one thing, but Moses starts talking back to the bush, which makes it another thing. You are either dehydrated or this is a moment where God is present, clearly. He tells him to take off his sandals because the place that he is standing is holy ground. Moses takes off his sandals and God makes a statement to him, saying, "I want you to go down into Egypt and tell him to let my people go. Tell Pharaoh let my people go" (Exodus 9:1). Moses responds that there is no way I can go do that and God says something that is miraculous. He says, do not worry about it I am going with you.

Is there anybody reading this book besides me that if God told you to do something and then he said that he is the one going with you, that would be enough for you to go. God if you are going with me, I am going, well amen! For God does not call those who are qualified, but he qualifies those who he has called.

Jesus was on the Mountain with Peter, James, and John. The only time it is lonely at the top is when you choose to climb the mountain alone and see the dangerous thing about it. Living in isolation, after a while, it may not just be God that is talking to you. There is another spirit that comes to talk to you, such as demonic spirits but you need to be the one to realise and understand the voices that are speaking to you. You must tap into the prophetic for you to understand what spirit is speaking to you at that time because you are your own prophet. God wants to speak to you to elevate you.

Christians are finding it deeply unsettling to be told they cannot gather, cannot pray, and sing together as one voice. They find it especially disturbing, that they cannot take communion together during this period of COVID-19, which is a time of isolation. That is not to say we do not understand the precautions in the time of this viral pandemic. With few exceptions, and with heavy hearts, religious leaders of all major traditions are complying with government efforts to "flatten the curve" of the virus so it does not spread quickly and unmanageably. Nevertheless, there are at least two things Christians can contemplate that offer some measure of solace and comfort and turn this Lenten trial into renewal. First, rediscover the fact that Christians are not strangers to being separated. Second, cultivate a deeper understanding of the terrible power of isolation, an understanding that can prepare us for trials to come.

There is an arrogant spirit, which seeks to pretend things are simply fine when they are far from okay. Christians learn early on to put on a good face through their trials and tests because at the end of the day no one is going through it with you except God. But a good face is a put-on face. A church of masks is cold. The lonely isolated sheep shake hands and smile quietly as they shuffle out the door.

If you are socially isolated by God, please plan to do everything you can to change your situation to get to your elevation. Do not worry if you do not know what to do about it. The most important thing you can do is to ask God for help. He cares for you. If you would like me to pray for you, I will. **"If any of you lack wisdom,** let him ask of God, that giveth to all men liberally, and does not find fault; and it shall be given him" (James 1:5)

Chapter 3

We Are All Strangers in a Strange Land

S uch isolation happened right from the beginning of the world creation. Consider that the Apostle Paul was imprisoned just some 30 years after the establishment of the church at Pentecost. Although separated and isolated from his flocks, he wrote to them in prison and encouraged them to strengthen one another through the trials. Then came the Roman persecutions, and on through the ages. In the modern era, persecution of Christians, as well as of Jews, have also been intense.

Here is a question that we must ask ourselves: What is God willing and able to do to bring us back to him? You might have decided to leave God because you have thoughtlessly drifted from him or you may have continually and consciously disobeyed him by committing a variety of sins, which God does not like or what may be displeasing to him. Nevertheless, you must wonder what is God willing to do now within your life? Those that desire to see God move mightily in their lives and within the church that they worship him under must be able to acknowledge the truth that God is willing and will to do whatever it takes to bring us back to him in order for him to get the glory and our souls to be saved.

As we look closer at Jonah within the bible, we can begin to see ourselves or certain areas of our lives within his story. Saints, if you have come to the realisation that your spiritual fire, which God has placed upon you is slowly going out, then it is simply because you have chosen to live a life of outright rebellion against God and God is not pleased with your way of living. If you have purpose within Christ and you become disobedient and refuse to follow Gods instructions, then you should know that God will make sure that you fulfil his works. He has many ways to get our attention.

You need to ask yourself if you ever feel like you are slowly losing your fire or you are becoming disobedient to God, what is he willing to do? Within this story of Jonah, we see the five signs and actions that God uses to awaken us from our spiritual indifference or disobedience, which dwells within us. We must understand that it is important to remember that these actions, which God has used and put into place are intended for us as a correction, not a punishment. The story about Jonah shows us that he was heading in the wrong direction both physically and spiritually. So, God decided to intervene to turn him around so that Jonah could find his way back to him.

As the story begins to unfold piece by piece, we realise that we seem to not miss the interaction between God and Jonah. God decides to match every move that Jonah choses to make with a counter move of correction. Now saints, if you consider this you can see that we use the same strategy as Jesus when we play the well-known game called "Chess". Chess is a board game, which is played by two players using strategic skill. It is played on a chequered board on which each player moves the playing piece according to precise rules. The object is to put the opponent's king under a direct attack from which escape is impossible. Once this is accomplished, the winner will then be declared, and the phrase Checkmate will be heard.

For you to fulfil your God given purpose, God may choose to send storms into your life (Jonah 1:4).

The text from within the passage tells us, "The Lord hurled a violent wind." The Hebrew term translated "hurled" or "flung" is the same word used when King Saul "cast" the javelin at young David. The word carries the description of "violent force." Here we see that the wind and waves served as God's servants to disturb the sleeping prophet.

God often uses the storms of adversity to teach us or to correct us. This storm illustrated the spiritual struggle of Jonah's heart. While the rebellious prophet knew what was right, a fierce battle raged in his soul.

God's goal in affliction is to awaken us and our spirits. When analysing Jonah life, character, and mission within the scripture and attributing the same to ourselves, we see that sometimes God must shake us to awaken us. Physically and figuratively, this storm was sent for Jonah. And we see God use this method of correction many times in the Bible. Jacob's deception was followed by the deception of his father-in-law. The Israelites refused to seize the promise land and were forced to wander in the wilderness for 40 years. Sampson lost his eyes and spent the rest of his days pushing a grindstone like a donkey. And King David had to run from his own son. While these storms come into our lives for many reasons, we should always ask,

"God, what are you trying to tell me through this trial?" "God what do you want me to learn from this lesson?" and "God why do I have to go through this?"

He touches someone near you (Jonah 1:5). Although Jonah had sinned, "the sailors were afraid." Our sins will certainly get ourselves in trouble with God and man, but it will get others in trouble too.

When the storm had come along, Jonah was about to drown. But remember, no one drowns alone. The storms that God had put into action touched his life and touched the lives of all those around him. After King David's sin, he remained in an unrepentant state for nearly a year. You might recall that after about eight months the prophet Nathan confronted David. And Nathan told David that the child born of the king's adultery would die. God touched the child to get David's attention. You should consider the answer to this question, what is God willing to do to bring you back to him? The answer is: whatever it takes! God knows which nerve to touch to get your attention

He touches you physically (Jonah 1:15). Once they had learned of Jonah's guilt "they picked up Jonah and threw him into the sea."

What does this mean theologically? It means that God's hand of protection can become his hand of correction. Do you remember the Israelites wandering around in the wilderness? When they turned on Moses and complained about God, the Lord sent snakes into the camp and many died (Numbers 21). It is interesting that up until that time, a million people wandered through that snake infested land without record of one bite. Then God removed his hand of protection as an act of correction.

Chapter 4

God desires
to awaken our spirit

Why would God use seemingly drastic intervention to get our attention? Is God mad at us? Does He desire to punish us? No! His correction is another expression of His love grace and goodness. He wants you back and hates the damage that sin brings to your life. So, He works to awaken us spiritually. Specifically, as the Lord has purposes for our life within his correction:

God desires for us to acknowledge his presence (Jonah 1:10). Jonah ran "from the presence of God." But God wanted him back.

God desires for us to acknowledge our sin (Jonah 1:9-10). We know that Jonah offered a public confession, "for he had told them." "Unconfessed sin is a weight which no wing can lift; it is a darkness that no light can banish; it is a disease that no medicine can cure." If we acknowledge that sin is our problem, then having an honest confession is the remedy or the solution to that problem (1 John 1:9).

God desires for us to submit to his will (Jonah 1:2). God told Jonah to "Go to Nineveh." Obedience to the Lord's command will bring an end to his correction. We should notice that the call to Nineveh did not change, meaning that once God has a plan or a work for you to fulfil no matter how many sins you commit at the end of the day you will still have to fulfil it as God personally chose you for the job because you have a purpose within you (Jonah 3:1).

God requires genuine repentance

How should we respond to God's loving motivations? I like how Max Lucado has put it: "If there are 1,000 steps between you and God, God will take 999 of them and leave the last one for you." God wants you to come back to him, but you must take a step toward him. That step is called repentance, which means going to God sincerely with all your heart and truthfully, crying out to him from the depth of your being, telling him that you are sorry for the wrongs that you have done.

When god speaks

Children of God, how many times has the Lord spoken to us and we have decided to turn a deaf ear or even a blind eye? If you choose to be honest with your response then you would probably say, 'a lot of times'. The book of Job confirms within chapter 33:14 where it reads, "For God does speak–now one way, now another–though no one perceives it"

There are many people within this world that love to play the blame game and may choose to ask questions like, 'When did God say something, and we did not listen or take heed?" So, in other words, there are some people that think that God does not speak to them and does not show them signs like he does with others who claim to have heard from him or he has shown them visons.

If you would, please allow me to portray various methods by which God speaks to us and we tend not to understand that it is he that is speaking to us. Human beings are naturally spiritual and therefore want something to keep the spiritual part satisfied. I want to declare today to you that, the spiritual part is God's part that is largely abused by the devil with false and unsatisfying spiritual things. God's part in the human spirit can only be satisfied by him. Psalm 16:1 tells us, "You make known to me the path of life; in your presence there is fullness of joy; at your right hand are pleasures forevermore."

I will now show you the type of ways by which God speaks to us today:

- ✓ The conscience. It is put by God in every individual to give personal guidance to every living individual. That is why you hear people say things like, 'I felt like what I was about to do or say was not good', even when others feel like it would not have been an issue doing it. The conscience works one-on-one, and its message is final. Once your conscience condemns you on something, know that it is God telling you and not necessarily your conscience.

- ✓ The Word of God, which is the Holy Bible. The word of God is shared in all forms of communication that are in the world today. Whoever claims not to have heard from the Word of God is telling a lie. The Word is on the internet, radio, television, word of mouth, newspapers, magazines, notice boards, books, etc.

✓ There are many that choose to question the Holy Bible and its contents. I suggest they test the divinity of the Holy Bible through their conscience.

All scripture is given by inspiration of God, and is profitable for doctrine, for reproof, for correction, for instruction in righteousness: That the man of God may be perfect, thoroughly furnished unto all good works (2 Timothy 3:16-17).

So therefore, I strongly suggest they consider their conscience and convictions on anything and then test it through insights sourced from the Holy Bible. It will not be difficult to soon realise that the Holy Bible does not contradict with what the conscience says. You can try this method of testing even with other religious books such as the Quran in which you would see that the sources within the Holy Bible are accurate.

✓ God speaks to people through dreams and visions. Job 33:15 says, "He speaks in dreams, in visions of the night, when deep sleep falls on people as they lie in their beds". This is one controversial way by which God speaks. He committed that in the last days he will use this method (Acts 2:17). Unfortunately, many false teachings have been founded on dreams and revelations that are not of God. This can imply that all dreams and visions that may be shared in any way should be tested through the Holy Bible. If the Bible confirms the message of the dreams and visions say, then it is a message coming from God. Another method of testing dreams and visions to know if they are of God or of the devil. What you will have to do is to call the name of Jesus upon them. A vision that will not fall off at the mention of the name of Jesus proves to be of God. There are many sources of dreams and visions, particularly those documented in forms of books, sermons, and audio files. Many of them contradict with each other, yet the best of all is one that is in line with what the Holy Bible says. I have heard so many of them online and I can tell you that there are those that come from the devil, which people promote without being careful to test them. A typical example of devil given vision is through websites and media platforms.

✓ God speaks through other people. People are most often God's messengers, sometimes without even knowing it. Have you ever gotten advice that suited your soul such that you do not have to question it or why you are receiving this message now, in time? When people give their testimonies whether in church or elsewhere, it is one way of letting God speak through the lives of others on how wonderful he is to mankind. God uses people to speak to us such as Pastors, Prophets, Evangelists, Prophetess, Apostles,

Bishops, family members or even your brothers and sisters within Christ.

✓ God often chooses to send His angels to us to guide us. This is one method by which God speaks with actions. Some guidance given unto you can and may be confusing towards the human mind, but we need to understand and realise that when it is the Lord's doing, his will and way will always prevail. God gives people testimonies in church, where they testify and tell us how they have felt a physical touch at the right time whether to save them from danger or for comfort. Some angels will manifest in the physical form, that is, as humans but for the man who gets the message often does not realise it until later after thinking on it.

I encourage you all to talk to God freely as you would do with a friend in the physical world. Communicate with him. Tell him about your troubles and tell him how you are feeling at any given point. I suggest you ask God to talk to you in a way that will let you understand and believe that it is him speaking to you. God is faithful and just to grant you your request if it is appropriate and accurate according to his will.

To conclude, at the end of the day, God speaks in a way that you will understand and not doubt it. To me he speaks with a combination of all the five, but I make sure to test each message by using the name of Jesus Christ.

When God speaks and you know that it is him speaking and you choose to ignore the message, your resistance to his word makes him very unhappy and he is forced to correct you. I encourage you to do what he says and do not be glued to things of this world.

What shall it profit a man if he gains the whole world and loose his soul? (Mark 8:36).

What God will do to you?

What God will do is isolate and separate you for you to be elevated. He will separate you from the familiar to the unfamiliar, comfortable to uncomfortable, friends, family, places, ministry, and the environment. Be ye separate

"Be ye not unequally yoked together with unbelievers: for what fellowship hath righteousness with unrighteousness? and what communion hath light with darkness? And what concord hath Christ with Belial? or what part hath he that believeth with an infidel? And what agreement hath the temple of God with idols? for ye are the temple of the living God; as God hath said, I will dwell in them, and walk in them; and I will be their God, and they shall be my people. Wherefore come out from among them, and be ye separate, saith the Lord, and touch not the unclean thing; and I will receive you, and will be a Father unto you, and ye shall be my sons and

daughters, saith the Lord Almighty" (2 Corinthians 6:14–18)

"And be not conformed to this world: but be ye transformed by the renewing of your mind, that ye may prove what is that good, and acceptable, and perfect, will of God" (Romans 12:2)

Be ye separate. When we look throughout the bible, we can see that separation runs throughout it. There are only two sides of separation, one that decides to serve God and surrender all their life to him totally and completely, and one that chooses to serve the devil. Those who serve God are the ones that have chosen to leave behind anything of this world and what it has to offer that would separate them from Jesus. Those who love and follow the ways of the ungodly world around them have chosen a different path. Today, in the very last days, it is of the biggest necessity that we know which side we are on. For to choose to be partly on the side of the world is to be completely an alien and stranger to the side of Christ.

Today's separation and isolation from churchgoing should also remind Christians of ultimate isolation: separation from God. The starkest definition of sin is separation from God, and it is in that separation that we founder and lay waste to ourselves and others. That is why imposed separation, the sort that is intended to weaken and hurt others, is evil.

These extraordinary circumstances should also remind us that in our faith, we are never alone. God is always with us. To build that consciousness of our Creator's presence is to be home, to be known and loved, and not to be a stranger. When we lose the privilege of worshiping in person with our brothers and sisters in Christ, we feel homesickness.

It is especially important that we as Christians separate ourselves from the world, its values, practices, and influences. Any concept that encourages slackness of Christian principles in this area is like a needle that deflates the balloon of the entire Christian experience.

In fact, the very biblical definition of a Christian is one who has separated from the sinful ways of the world.

"A Christian, as described by the Scriptures, is a person who is separated from the world in his aims and practices and is united with Christ, a possessor of the peace and ensures to uphold the standard and characteristics of God, which Christ alone can bestow, finding that the joy of the Lord is his strength and that his joy is full." In Heavenly Places, "those who decide to leave the world by joining the covenant with God in the spirit and in all practice may regard themselves as sons and daughters of God."

In other words, God's followers are only those who are willing and ready to leave the world behind to serve him in every way. Those who still grasp to the things and ways of the world with one hand, as Lot's wife did, unwilling to give them up, these people are not Gods sons and daughters. In fact, our separation from the ways of the world is a thermometer of the depth of our Christian experience. So, those who isolate and separate themselves from the world behind and the things of the world such as the flashy lifestyle, fame and popularity offered by the devil will be elevated both physically and spiritually in God and gain the harvest of Deuteronomy 28 blessings.

There are conditions to meet if we would be blessed and honoured by God. We are to be separate from the world and refuse to touch those things that will separate our affections from God.

Chapter 5

The Wrath of God

I think we all think of something awful when we hear or think of the word wrath and we are correct to have that reaction. So, let use examine the word more closely.

What Is Wrath?

There are a few words in both the Old and New Testaments that are translated as the wrath of God. These words are also often translated as anger. Usually they are referring to God's response to human disobedience, but the words are also used in relation to a negative human response to other people. There is no good way to soften "the wrath of God" to mean anything other than an angry response on God's part to human disobedience.

The wrath of God is a common example in the Old Testament. Deuteronomy 9:8 is an example of this usage, "At Horeb you aroused the Lord's wrath so that he was angry enough to destroy you." This combination of God's wrath, human disobedience, and punishment is a common theme in the Old Testament, especially in the prophets. The primary message of the prophets was one of the judgments against a disobedient person, typically with a call for repentance.

There are also dozens of references to God's wrath in the New Testament, including Romans 1:18, "The wrath of God is being revealed from heaven against all the godlessness and wickedness of people, who suppress the truth by their wickedness." Even though Jesus and his disciples proclaimed the kingdom of God, and expressed God's love for humanity, they did not dismiss the wrath of God. Wrath that would come to all who were disobedient to the gospel message.

Each of us desires to be a son or daughter of the most high, and God mercifully makes known to us how we can cooperate with the work he wants to do in us. He has not left us to stumble in the dark, seeking for acceptance with God. Instead, He has made the conditions plain, and one of them, an especially important one, is separation from the world. The condition of our acceptance with God is a practical separation from the world.

Practically speaking, what is separation from the world, and how separate are we to be? This revolves around our upholding and living the Law of God, which is trodden down by those around us. It involves our believing and teaching the great message of truth committed to us by God in His Word. And, just as importantly, it involves our living out this truth in our daily lives. Our daily lives must be in wide contrast to the habits and customs of those around us.

We are not to elevate our standard just a little above the world's standard, but we are to make the distinction decidedly apparent. The reason we have had so little influence upon unbelieving relatives and associates is that there has been so little decided difference between our practices and those of the world.

In the service of God there is no middle ground. **"Let none expect to make a compromise with the world, and yet enjoy the blessing of the Lord. Let God's people come out from this world and be separate."Matt. 12:30**

Who Will Experience God's Wrath?

Throughout the Scriptures within the Bible, God's wrath is earmarked for those who are in rebellion against him. But the wrath is never the experience of those who are responsive to his call. Believers may, and do, experience discipline from the hand of God. But that discipline is put into place to help us to grow and mature us in the faith of God, and in relationship that we have or should have with God to be elevated and empowered within him. Wrath is the final judgment against all those who are accounted as God's enemies, those who have turned their faces away from God.

All of this is a powerful reminder that Christians have nothing to fear. To have faith is to set aside anxieties and depression and to put our trust in the grand plan in which we do our best as servants of Christ.

Throughout the Scriptures and stories in the Bible, you will find that this division between God's wrath directed towards sinners and his protecting love toward his own. His wrath is poured out on the people of Noah's day by the waters of the flood, but righteous Noah and his family are rescued. Judgment is levied against Sodom and Gomorrah and Lot is rescued. Egypt is destroyed by the plagues while the descendants of Abraham are delivered. Over and over we see this repeated in the Old Testament. And that same story is also vividly portrayed in the visions of John recorded in Revelation.

- ✓ **Romans 1:18 -** For the wrath of God is revealed from heaven against all ungodliness and unrighteousness of men, who by their unrighteousness suppress the truth.

✓ **John 3:36 -** Whoever believes in the Son has eternal life; whoever does not obey the Son shall not see life, but the wrath of God remains on him.

✓ **Romans 12:17 -** Repay no one evil for evil but give thought to do what is honourable in the sight of all. If possible, so far as it depends on you, live peaceably with all. Beloved, never avenge yourselves, but leave it to the wrath of God, for it is written, "Vengeance is mine, I will repay, says the Lord." To the contrary, "if your enemy is hungry, feed him; if he is thirsty, give him something to drink; for by so doing you will hear burning coals on his head." Do not be overcome by evil but overcome evil with good.

✓ **Ezekiel 25:17 -** I will execute great vengeance on them with wrathful rebukes. Then they will know that I am the Lord when I lay my vengeance upon them.

✓ **Isaiah 26:21 -** For behold, the Lord is coming out from his place to punish the inhabitants of the earth for their iniquity, and the earth will disclose the blood shed on it and will no more cover its slain.

✓ **Nahum 1:2-6 -** The Lord is a jealous and avenging God; the Lord is avenging and wrathful; the Lord takes vengeance on his adversaries and keeps wrath for his enemies. The Lord is slow to anger and great in power, and the Lord will by no means clear the guilty. His way is in whirlwind and storm, and the clouds are the dust of his feet. He rebukes the sea and makes it dry; he dries up all the rivers; Bashan and Carmel wither; the bloom of Lebanon withers. The mountains quake before him; the hills melt; the earth heaves before him, the world and all who dwell in it. Who can stand before his indignation? Who can endure the heat of his anger? His wrath is poured out like fire, and the rocks are broken into pieces by him.

✓ **Psalm 7:11 -** God is a righteous judge, and a God who feels indignation every day.

✓ **Matthew 10:28 -** And do not fear those who kill the body but cannot kill the soul. Rather fear him who can destroy both soul and body in hell.

✓ **Revelation 19:11-21 -** Then I saw heaven opened, and behold, a white horse! The one sitting on it is called Faithful and True, and in righteousness he judges and makes war. His eyes are like a flame of fire, and on his head are many diadems, and he has a name written that no one knows but himself. He is clothed in a robe dipped in blood, and the name by which he is called is The Word of God. And the armies of heaven, arrayed in fine linen, white and pure, were following him on white horses. From his mouth comes a sharp sword with which to strike down the nations, and he will rule them with a rod of iron. He will tread the winepress of the fury of the wrath of God the Almighty.

✓ **2 Peter 2:9 -** Then the Lord knows how to rescue the godly from trials, and to keep the unrighteous under punishment until the day of judgment,

✓ **Revelation 20:15 -** And if anyone has name was not found written in the book of life, he was thrown into the lake of fire.

✓ **Romans 6:23 -** For the wages of sin is death, but the gift of God is eternal life in Christ Jesus our Lord.

✓ **Romans 2:5 -** But because of your hard and impenitent heart you are storing up wrath for yourself on the day of wrath when God's righteous judgment will be revealed.

✓ **Romans 5:9 -** Since, therefore, we have now been justified by his blood, much more shall we be saved by him from the wrath of God

The anger of God is not like our anger

When we are isolated and we still do not fulfil Gods work and will, we cannot be elevated, which will make God angry and maybe even pour out his wrath on us to show us that he is God and his will must be carried out.

When we speak about the wrath of God, remember that it is the wrath of God and not the anger of man. So, everything we know about God, he is just, he is love, and he is good, needs to be poured into our understanding of his wrath.

The words "anger" and "wrath" make us think about our own human experience. You may have suffered because of someone, maybe a girlfriend, boyfriend, husband, wife, or an enemy whom you thought was a friend, who is usually angry, loses their temper, or flies into a rage.

Our anger can often be unpredictable, petty, and disproportionate.

Although these things are often true of human anger, none of them are true of the anger of God. God's wrath is the just and measured response of his holiness towards evil.

God's wrath is provoked

The anger of God is not something that resides in him by nature; it is a response to evil. It is provoked.

The Bible says, "God is love." That is his nature. God's love is not provoked. He does not love us because he sees some wisdom, beauty, or goodness in us. He loves you because he loves you, and you can never get beyond that (Deuteronomy 7:7). And so therefore the reason why God chooses to isolate you is to elevate you because he loves you and wants the best for and out of you.

But God's wrath is different, his holy response to the intrusion of evil into his world. If there was no sin in the world, there would be no wrath in God. So, the Bible's teaching about the wrath of God is different from ancient mythologies. God's anger is settled resolve that evil will not stand.

"Will separation from the world, in obedience to the divine command, unfit us for the work the Lord has left us? Will it hinder us from doing good to those around us? No; the firmer hold we have on heaven, the greater will be our power of usefulness" (In Heavenly Places, 312). God would not so clearly command us to separate ourselves from this world's way of living if it were not for the best good of the upbuilding of His kingdom. In fact, the reason we have had so little influence upon unbelieving relatives and associates is that we have manifested little decided difference in our practices from those of the world.

God is slow to anger

Why does God allow evil to continue in the world? Why does he not wipe it out?

God holds out the offer of grace and forgiveness in Jesus Christ (2 Peter 3:9). People are coming to him in faith and repentance every day, and God patiently holds open the door of grace in the hope that people will change to know him better. In this they can move from a place of isolation of sin to elevation of righteousness. The day of God's wrath will come, but God is not in a hurry to bring it because then the door of grace will be closed.

God's wrath is revealed now

How does God reveal his wrath when sinners suppress the truth about him, exchange the truth for a lie, and worship created things rather than the Creator? God gives them up (Romans 1):

"Therefore, God gave them up in the lusts of their hearts to impurity" (Romans 1:24)

For this reason, God gave them up to dishonourable passions (Romans 1:26)

God gave them up to a debased mind (Romans 1:28)

One writer states "Paul is not teaching that one-day God will punish Roman civilization for its vice and decadence. On the contrary, the vice and decadence are themselves God's punishment. Their punishment was their greed, envy, strife, deceit, violence, and faithlessness" (2). When we see the moral fabric of our culture being torn, then as Christian believers we should cry out to God for mercy.

God's wrath is stored up

The whole Bible story leads to a day when God will deal with all evil fully, finally, and forever. This will be the day of wrath when God will recompense every evil and bring to judgment every sin.

God will do this in perfect justice. The punishment for every sin will match the crime. When the judgment is done, every mouth will be stopped because everyone will know that God judged in righteousness and justice. Then God will usher in a new heaven and a new earth, which will be the home of righteousness and elevation and not a place of separation.

God's wrath is on sinners

In John 3:36, he does not say, the wrath of God will come on the disobedient. He says, "Whoever does not obey the Son shall not see life, but the wrath of God remains on him." It is already there. Why is it already there? By nature, we are children of wrath (Ephesians 2:3). It is the state in which we were born.

What, at the end of the day, is the greatest human problem? It is not that we are lost and need to find our way on a spiritual journey. It is not that we are wounded and need to be healed. At the core of the human problem is that we are sinners under the judgment of God, and the divine wrath hangs over us unless and until it is taken away.

How God's Wrath Is Removed

The Bible speaks about God's wrath being poured out at the cross: "I will soon pour out my wrath upon you and spend my anger against you" (Ezekiel 7:8). This takes us to the heart of what happened there: the divine wrath toward sin was poured out on Jesus. He became the "propitiation" for our sins (Romans 3:25), which means that the payment for our sins was poured out on Jesus at Calvary.

Some people believe that Christians are not supposed to have emotional problems when in fact some Christians do. Believers in the Lord Jesus Christ are just as fallen as other people. Jesus showed us an example of this happening when he was carrying the cross, he fell several times, Jesus did not have any sins, but he took on the sins of the world through forgiveness. "For all have sinned and come short of the glory of God" (Romans 3:23). "And the scribes and Pharisees brought unto him a woman taken in adultery; and when they had set her in the midst, they say unto him, Master, this woman was taken in adultery, in the very act. Now Moses in the law commanded us, that such should be stoned: but what sayest thou? This they said, tempting him, that they might have to accuse him. But Jesus stooped down, and with his finger wrote on the ground, as though he heard them not. So when they continued asking him, he lifted up himself, and said unto them, He that is without sin among you, let him first cast a stone at her" (John 8:3-7). God makes his strength and love perfect in weakness. So, saint of God, ask God for forgiveness of your sins during your isolation so that those who laugh at you will be the same ones to see Gods hand upon your life when he strengthens and elevates you.

God makes his strength perfect in weakness It may be that we who take on the name of Christ have more issues than other people. As Jesus said, they that are whole have no need of the physician, but they that are sick: I came not to call the righteous, but sinners to repentance (Mark 2:17). St. Paul confirms it: For ye see your calling, brethren, how that not many wise men after the flesh, not many mighty, not many noble, are called: But God hath chosen the foolish things of the world to confound the wise; and God hath chosen the weak things of the world to confound the things which are mighty (1 Corinthians 1:26-27).

When we are faced with difficult situations it is not to destroy us, but it is to build us, to motivate us to become better version of ourselves. God has given us all a mandate as individuals and sometimes God must remove us from our comfort zone to introduce us to our destiny, introduce us to our God given calling. Some of us are too comfortable where we are at and we are not being as effective as we must be when we are truly operating in our divine calling. When we are walking in our God given destiny, that is when we are most effective. That is when we discover that which God has placed within us. Many of us has many gifts that God wants us to use for his kingdom in helping to build it, others, and even ourselves for the greater good of the kingdom manifestation.

Do not ever get the idea that God does not love you because you are in your problems, trials, and isolations or that you cannot hear from him or see him at that current moment. You need to be reminded that isolation brings elevation. Christ died for you because God loves you dearly! He loved you even when you were the object of his wrath! God so loved the objects of his wrath that he spent the wrath on himself when he died on the cross.

The outpouring of God's wrath was the greatest act of love this world has ever seen

The hope for sinners is that between us and the wrath of God stands the cross of Jesus. Sin was laid on Jesus and the divine wrath toward it was poured out, spent, and exhausted in the darkness of Calvary. And when it was done, Jesus cried out in a loud voice, "It is finished!" The wrath of God that will one day be poured out on sinners and all sin was spent on the cross regarding all who are in him. Then Christ rose from the dead, and he stands before you today, a living Saviour! He offers to you the priceless gift of peace with God. He is ready to forgive your sins and fill you with his Spirit and all the gifts he placed inside of you. He can save you from the wrath and reconcile you to the Father. He has opened the door of heaven, and he is able to bring you in.

DIVINE UPLIFTMENT

I waited patiently for the LORD; He turned to me and heard my cry. He lifted me out of the slimy pit, out of the mud and mire; He set my feet on a rock and gave me a firm place to stand.

He put a new song in my mouth, a hymn of praise to our God. Many will see and fear and put their trust in the LORD.

Blessed is the man who makes the LORD his trust, who does not look to the proud, to those who turn aside to false gods.

Many, O LORD my God, are the wonders you have done. The things you planned for us no one can recount to you; were I to speak and tell of them, they would be too many to declare.

This was a Psalm of David to declare the Praise of the Lord. We would remember that David was the most likely candidate who could have sang a song like this.

Another example of spiritual upliftment happened in the case of Mephibosheth in 2 Samuel 9:1-12. He was supposed to be a crown prince, but evil started trailing him when he was young. His name meant: "exterminator of shame" but as you can find in 2 Samuel 4:4, he was not crippled from his birth. He became a product of accident and then he became crippled. The Lord will defend your home, your children and all you have this year and for ever more in the name of Jesus. He became a victim of what he knew nothing about; but the Lord remembered him and brought him out of a forgotten land. From Lode bar, the Lord brought him out and he made him sit with the King at table. The Lord will remember you in the name of Jesus.

If you look at the book 2 Samuel 21: 1-7, the Bible also described how Mephibosheth was spared from death even when all the sons of Saul were killed in disgraceful circumstances. That happened because there was a severe famine in the land for three odd years. Even as we witness famine at this time within the bible, the Lord will keep you and even make you sit with Kings in the name of Jesus. The lesson I have learned since the beginning of this year, is that divine manifestation is always followed by divine upliftment and that will be our portion in the mighty name of Jesus. When God shows up in the case of a man, the man is always uplifted.

In the case of David, as he sang in the Book of Psalms 40: 1-5, he waited patiently for the Lord and the Lord inclined unto him and heard his cry. Subsequently, the Lord blessed him with five distinct blessings:

✓ The Lord turned toward him. That means that the Lord manifested himself in his affair. The Lord showed interest in his affairs and decided to get involved. That is divine manifestation. I have good news for you: The Lord is interested in your affairs. The Lord is interested in your matter. The Lord is interested in your life in a positive way.

✓ The Lord heard him (v. 1). When the Lord decides to hear you, it is wonderful! Psalms 20: 1-9 is truly clear about what it means for the Lord to hear us from his holy hill. This month as you wait upon the Lord in prayer, the Lord will hear your entire cry in the name of Jesus.

✓ He brought him out of the pit (Psalm 40:2). The most vivid example of a man in the pit was Joseph. He was taken out of the pit and he later became a Prime Minister. Such will be your elevation in the name of Jesus.

✓ He was also brought out of miry clay (Psalm 40:2). A commentator has described this as: "The great distress and trouble that the psalmist had been in the pit. He had been plunged into a horrible pit and into miry clay (Psalm 40:2), out of which he could not work himself, and in which he found himself sinking yet further. He says nothing here either of the sickness of his body or the insults of his enemies, and therefore we have reason to think it was some inward disquiet and perplexity of spirit that was now his greatest grievance. Despondency of spirit under the sense of God's withdrawing, and prevailing doubts and fears about the eternal state, are indeed a horrible pit and miry clay, and have been so to many a dear child of God."

✓ The Lord set his feet on the solid rock (Psalm 40:2). The Lord took him out of doubt and engrained him in his son. The Lord planted him in the cliffs of the Rock of Ages. That is a place where we can never be moved by the trials of life and the vagrancies of life.

✓ The Lord established his ways (Psalm 40:2). The Lord will establish your ways this year in the name of Jesus. Everything that represents impossibility in your life is turning to possibility in the name of Jesus.

✓ Finally, the Lord will put a new song in your mouth in the name of Jesus (Psalm 40:3). The Lord will turn your mourning into joy in the name of Jesus. The Lord will change your testimony in the name of Jesus.

That is what it means to be divinely uplifted!

Psalms 75:6-7, Esther 6:10-11.

WHAT DO WE MEAN BY DIVINE UPLIFTMENT?

✓ Divine upliftment is when a supernatural reward comes your way.

✓ Divine upliftment is when God takes you from zero to hero.

✓ Divine upliftment is to go beyond those that had earlier gone beyond you.

- ✓ Divine upliftment is when you have and are enjoying divine recognition.

- ✓ Divine upliftment is when you rise above your equals.

It is when you are taken out of many for honour.

The entire world is divided into four parts, North, South, East and West. In all segments of this world, there is none of them that can offer divine upliftment. Divine upliftment is never of this world, it only comes from God. As good as Western world is, the Bible says divine upliftment cannot come from there according to our golden text. But Mordecai enjoyed this divine upliftment from God, and that is telling us of our inheritance in the Lord as a believer. As Mordecai was lifted, so also with every believer that can function as he did. We are not to operate in the valley but to reign and rule in every area of our lives.

No matter who you are, lifting is your portion, and once you are a believer, lifting is always a great part of your journey you . Mordecai was a simple gatekeeper, but he was lifted to be the vice president of a nation. That also took place in a strange land. He was a Jew living in Babylon as a slave unto others, but still experienced divine upliftment. Once you are a believer, location is never a barrier to your uplifting. Wherever you find yourself, lifting from God is there with you. But lifting from God cannot just takes place, there are secrets to it. If you want God to lift you there are things to learn from the lifting of Mordecai. Mordecai was lifted because he had God. That was the reason he could not bow down to any man. Haman wanted him to bow down for him, and as a Jew, Mordecai was not to bow down for any other thing but God alone. You will need God to experience divine upliftment.

Mordechai was lifted just because he chose not to violate the word of God, Exodus 20:4-6. It was the commandment of God not to bow down for any other thing, and Mordecai choose to keep that commandment even at the expense of his life. You must keep the word and commandment of God if you are to be lifted and elevated in Christ.

Mordechai was lifted because he had a good work and testimony, Esther 6:1-2, Psalms 1:1. There is a need for you as a believer to have a work, for God to work out your divine upliftment. Your work will serve as a medium to work out your blessing, without work nothing resolves. The report, which was also recorded about Mordecai to work out his upliftment included that he had a good testimony before the king and others. When people are giving bad reports about you, it may really affect your upliftment.

Mordecai was lifted because he was faithful to the king, his boss. Loyalty pays. He did everything possible to safeguard the life of the king, he could not shut his mouth when he saw evil coming towards his boss. He was never walking in agreement with the wicked (Psalms 1:1). That loyalty came back to lift him beyond measure in a strange land. Mordechai was lifted because he did not take spiritual things with levity (Esther 4:15-

17). Mordecai was instructed to embark on spiritual disciplines to back up his cousin Esther and Jews. He was older than Esther and possibly had more understanding than she did, but he never looked down on her. He took the instruction very seriously and that later saved him and the Jews from the evil conspiracy of Haman.

Mordechai was lifted because he knew people in the palace (Esther 4:1-2). Divine upliftment at times cannot come until after you have an encounter with especially important people. There is always an agent of upliftment, which heaven had designed to take us to the promise land. Mordecai got the attention of the King because he had his cousin in the palace (Esther 2:22). It was that information the king was ruminating about, and that prompted the upliftment of Mordecai. Joseph also could not rise to the top until after he met Pharaoh's cup bearer in the prison. It was the cup bearer that mentioned Joseph to king Pharaoh and that really lifted Joseph to the top (Genesis 40:1-14, 41:9-14).

Mordecai was lifted because he was a man of fasting and prayer. Jesus said, there are things that will not be except we are very prayerful with fasting (Matthew 17:21). When Mordecai and the Jews heard what Haman had planned against them, they did not consult anyone but God first with fasting and prayer (Esther 4:1-3). One man of God said, "nothing lies beyond the reach of prayer, except one that lies outside the will of God". There is nothing to compare with fasting and prayer, it was the same weapon used by disciples to deliver Peter from the prison of Herod. It was their prayers that set Peter loose. It was prayer that brought down the angel from above and break every unbreakable chain (Acts 12:5-10). With prayer, there is no mountain you cannot reach if you believe.

He remained faithful to God even at the expense of his life. Standing up for God is not always easy as persecution will be set in place whenever you want to defend your faith by standing for the Lord Jesus Christ. This persecution has led many Christians to be living in compromise continuously, but Mordecai could not compromise his faith in a strange land. We have seen many believers turned to worship another thing when they travelled out of the country, and many students turned to prostitution when they received admission into tertiary institutions. But Mordecai compromise not his standing for God, even when it is difficult, Esther 3:4-6.

He had a job; he was a gate man. He was not a believer alone but engaged himself in doing something to take care of himself as well as his family. He was a man of faith but had to work on it, for the Bible says faith without works is dead (James 2:14-18).

You need a job where you will enjoy your divine upliftment, but your job is never enough. We have many with jobs but not lifted, just because they are never standing for God in their job, neither faithful to their boss as Mordecai was. Your work is a means for God to work out your divine upliftment and to grow you to become powerful. God does not support being idle so if you are maintaining idleness within you, cast out that spirit. Idleness at times can be a barrier to your upliftment.

FACTS ABOUT UPLIFTMENT

It is God alone that can work out divine upliftment and elevation within your life. Mordecai was never pushing for it, he just remained faithful to God and continued in his work.

There is always an agent of divine upliftment. It was the king that God used to lift Mordecai. You do not know who God will end up using for your upliftment and elevation. It could even be your enemies that God uses. If it was a bad report they wrote down for Mordecai, his lifting will have been difficult on that fateful day.

Someone must fall for you to rise. Two people cannot occupy or be in the same position at the same time.

Your post to conquer is not always far away. Some will never rise in life just because they have set their eyes on a particular post or position, which may prompt them in thinking evil against the occupant of that position. Mordecai did not eye the post, neither wish his boss evil (Psalm 24:3).

There is a higher place of the Lord, which is created only for people with clean hands and pure heart.

It is only the meek that God lifts up. If you are proud, your lifting will be difficult as we read in Psalms 147:6, "The LORD lifteth up the meek: he casteth the wicked down to the ground."

They that are proud can never experience the lifting of God. It is because it takes a spiritual and mature person not to misbehave at the top. Haman was carnal, that was why he fell from grace. I pray the Lord to help us all in Jesus name. Amen.

Elevate Your Life!

✓ **Ephesians 2:6 (NIV)** - "God raised us up with Christ and seated us with him in the heavenly realms in Christ Jesus."

- ✓ **Luke 9:1 (NIV) -** "When Jesus had called the Twelve together, he gave them power and authority to drive out all demons and to cure diseases."

- ✓ **Exodus 3:6 (NKJV) -** "Moreover He said, "I am the God of your father—the God of Abraham, the God of Isaac, and the God of Jacob." And Moses hid his face, for he was afraid to look upon God."

- ✓ **Exodus 3:9-10 (NKJV) -** "Now therefore, behold, the cry of the children of Israel has come to Me, and I have also seen the oppression with which the Egyptians oppress them. Come now, therefore, and I will send you to Pharaoh that you may bring My people, the children of Israel, out of Egypt".

Spiritual Elevation

Spiritual elevation happens because of the divine plan that God has for your life. Divine means it has been prepared by God in heaven but should happen here on earth. Your promotion does not start here but in the spirit first before it manifests in the flesh. God will arrange a divine setup that should happen on earth.

A setup is what God has organized and arranged for you. There are some people around you who will stop you within your isolation so that you do not reach your elevation. God does things according to his will and way and everything happens for a reason. Everyone who wants to go up should always be prepared to go down so that the enemies think that you have been destroyed. In spiritual elevation, there is laughter by people at first, even by your own friends and love ones so saints of God be prepared to face challenges.

Even if the struggle becomes overwhelming and real, you are more than a conqueror through Christ who strengthens you, as Philippians 4:13 reminds us that "I can do all things through Christ which strengtheneth me." There is a time for a prophecy and a time for fulfilment of that prophesy to come to pass in our lives.

Before the prophecy is fulfilled, you need to endure the pain that you feel in between so that when you have made it to that level of elevation from isolation, you will testify of the goodness of the Lord. **"Through desire a man, having separated himself, seeketh [and] intermeddleth with all wisdom" (Proverbs 18:1).**

Children of God, we need to understand that throughout the tough situations we may stumble upon during our Christian walk we need to remember that God will always have a plan for you and for your life, so instead of saying, "God why is this happening to me," you should be saying, "God what plans do you have for my life now." You will always survive evil works and death because God is by your side through thick and thin, when church sister and brother, friends and family were not there for you God was always there. You may not see him or hear him but believe that he is there.

"Fear thou not; for I am with thee be not dismayed; for I am thy God: I will strengthen thee; yea, I will

help thee; yea, I will uphold thee with the right hand of my righteousness" (Isaiah 41:10).

What was meant to destroy you will not. If you want to excel in life, you need to pray, fast, worship, and read the word to maintain a closer relationship with God. If you do not, you will not be a candidate for spiritual elevation but rather of isolation.

Let the isolated Christians remember the body of Christ to elevate. Each member has its function, we need you and you need us, neither of us can say we do not need the other. **"If the foot shall say, Because I am not the hand, I am not of the body; is it therefore not of the body? And if the ear shall say, Because I am not the eye, I am not of the body; is it therefore not of the body? If the whole body were an eye, where were the hearing? If the whole were hearing, where were the smelling? But now hath God set the members every one of them in the body, as it hath pleased him" (1 Corinthians 12:15-18).**

I doubt that you will find a church to meet your need in every aspect, but the church still needs you for God has placed a purpose upon your life for you to help others within the body of Christ and out of the body of Christ. If the church gathered on a scriptural basis then your ministry would be much better. Unfortunately, now people are missed for not filling the empty pews rather than for their ministry input. Do not put your trust in man, no matter how wonderful he seems at the time, he will only fail you or misunderstand you at the time you most need him to understand whereas God understands you at all times.

You should not do things to please people, church leaders, friends, or family but rather to please God and only God. Everything you do, do it for God. Do not allow pity from people; work for God because he is the rewarder and you shall receive the reward of the inheritance (Colossians 3:24). Surrender your life to God and he will lift you up and make a way for you despite you thinking that there is not a way. Some things happen so that the glory of the Lord is uplifted and seen. It is not every disadvantage that destroys you; some happen to your advantage.

He is only human so do not see him through rose tinted spectacles, neither lift him up in your own eyes as someone who you can put your trust in. Put your trust in the Lord not in your pastor. Your pastor will make mistakes so pray for him and love him. If we put our trust in man, we are setting ourselves up to be hurt. The bible says, "Cursed is the man that trusteth in man" (Jeremiah 17:5). In other words, things will go wrong for us if we trust in man. However, blessed is the man that puts his trust in the Lord (Jeremiah 17:7). It is the Lord we need to depend on, not man. When we go through hard and difficult times, that bring us to despair, it is because God is teaching us to trust in him and in him alone. "Despair is only cured at the point where we become fully aware of our own dependence on God" (From 'In Search of Personality' by Peter Morea, p. 43). If at these times of despair, we turn to man, putting our trust in him as a person to meet our need, then God will have to deal with us even more critically to teach us to put our faith solely in him. If only we would become fully dependent on God for everything rather than relying on man as a crutch because we do not trust the Lord in all our ways. Of course, there are some 'good' men who we can love and respect. We can trust them to do their absolute best not to let us down, however they are still human and can make mistakes or misunderstand us. We may trust their word while at the same time recognising their fallibility. We should not put our trust 'in' them as a person. That is reserved for God alone.

This is your hour to arise and shake off all restraints of bondage as the glory of the Lord now appears in your life. Fresh start, new beginning, restoration, redevelopment of your life health and finances has begun!

A Major Spiritual Elevation Is Taking Place

There is a major spiritual elevation taking place! This morning, my spirit is leaping and turning, the activity of worship that is springing forth from my inner man is in major manifestation. The atmosphere today is so heavy with newness and a travail of birthing is taking place. It has taken me into a deeper realm of respect for God. The splendour of his Glory and the awesomeness of his presence is pushing me into a greater intimacy. All I want, is to be consumed by him, engulfed in the fire of the Holy Ghost. I cannot even explain the magnitude of this feeling I am experiencing as his Spirit continues to overtake me at different times this morning.

Chapter 6

Choice God gave us the chance to choose again

I love the fact that God is always so forgiving, even when we are unworthy, he still leaves the door open for us. He gives us free will, John 7:17 is a great example of that as it says, "Anyone who chooses to do the will of God will find out whether my teaching comes from God or whether I speak on my own." It is clear that although God loves us, he does not take away our choice.

Being confident of this very thing, that he which hath begun a good work in you will perform it until the day of Jesus Christ (Philippians 1:6).

On different occasions throughout a variety of churches, there have been many sermons preached about a blind man who had lived in a town know as Bethsaida (Mark 8:22-25). There are many writings, which have been used such as "Look Again," "seeing again" "a new sight" or "Don't Give Up on What God Can Do," and "NEVER EVER GIVE UP." The truth is that God is continually drawing his people and making them understand that hope must never be lost, released, or abandoned within your walk with him. Hope is basically the anchor of the soul that ensures our stability within Christ and minimizes our destruction during the storms, so that we are sustained to move on and arrive at our purpose after the storm.

The relevance and meaning behind this story are not to inform and let us know that the man was blind, but that he was a human. And he received, just like most believers receive. His victory was not immediate, but it came through a process, which means that it took time. The process did more than make things better, it made things right. Always believe that it is the will of God to bring WHOLENESS and to become whole you have been isolated (process) to get victory (elevate).

The story goes as this, the first touch of Jesus made him better, but the second touch made him whole. Just release yourself to the process and trusting him knowing that he is always acting and leading with our best interest in mind. Do not think that just because he is putting you in a place of isolation that he is choosing to forget about you or overlook you. What he is doing is making you better both physically and spiritually.

Although the blind man's first look cancelled the darkness surrounding and drew in the light, he would have been left functionally crippled for the rest of his life. Crippled because defeat and discouragement would have been given a license to freely operate in a man who was already looking down (which most blind men do not do). Like the blind man, are you delivered but damaged? Are you dealing with the leftovers after deliverance? Tears and grief are gone, but now there is resentment, hardness, habits, and cravings. Never believe that the FIRST LOOK is the conclusion of the whole matter. The first look is an OPPORTUNITY to raise your level of expectation. The first look is the ASSURANCE that God never starts a job that he is not committed to finishing. It is God's gift for every citizen of the kingdom to know that whoever has, to him shall be given, and he shall have more abundance (Matthew 13:11-12). If God has done anything in your life, that is your evidence that there is always much more in store. God is not through blessing you! Look again! Get ready for the NEXT move of God! Get ready for the NEXT TOUCH of God! Look into the Word again! Believe God again! Complete restoration is possible. You can see clearly again. Without a doubt, the best is yet to come. And if you can say, he has begun a good work in me, SHOUT NOW, 'the best is yet to come after my isolation period.'

With the PEACE of God, with his RESURRECTION POWER, with his guidance as our SHEPHERD, and with his BLOOD that WASHES and CLEANSES us, the God of peace makes us perfect in every good work to do his will, working in us that which is well pleasing in his sight, through Jesus Christ (Hebrews 13:20-21). But the God of all grace, who hath called us unto his eternal glory by Christ Jesus, after that ye have suffered a while, make you perfect, establish, strengthen, settle you (1 Peter 5:10).

Give God Another Chance to Make It Right

Repositioning Our Receiver

"Cast not away therefore your confidence, which hath great recompense of reward. For ye have need of patience, that, after ye have done the will of God, ye might receive the promise" (Hebrews 10:35-36).

Every human being always deals with issues which are very much like the television of my childhood. We have the potential of a picture-perfect life. We have the potential of walking and living in the abundant life that Jesus came to provide. However, we often get discouraged by reflections with distortion, no clarity, and incompleteness. Jesus is the channel that we should be tuned into, but we will always miss the best that he can provide if we fail to receive or inconsistently or partially receive. What Jesus gives is always with maximum power and absolute clarity, but we fall short on the receiving end. He is always enough. And He is always exhorting us to make whatever adjustments are necessary to RECEIVE. So, saints, if you want to receive you need to go into isolation and you SHALL receive elevation.

Satan has no ability to stop or frustrate the purpose and the people of God. So, he decides to work on us during our time of isolation and even in our elevation so that we will let our trust in the Lord die and our fire burn out when simple or problematic things happen. We then end up giving up on our reward! We give up on what God has promised us for our lives. But let me tell you this, if we want to receive from God, if you want him to do for us all that he has promised, we need to keep on patiently doing God's will. His coming will not be delayed for much longer as we are in the last days. And those whose faith has made them good in God's sight must live by faith, trusting him in everything. Otherwise, if they shrink back, God will have no pleasure in them (Hebrews 10:35-38).

If I were asked to rank words in the New Testament in the order of importance, "Jesus" would be first, and "love" would be second. The third one would most likely be the word "receive." The God of this universe, which is Jesus Christ, has set in motion the principals of receiving. In fact, almost everything in life is affected by these principals. The crop in the field never grows except the ground receives the seed sown into the earth and it is watered. The farmer never stores or eats of the harvest without receiving it from the field. This is just like many of us within the church and the kingdom of God.

Almost every day today and especially during this isolation period of COVID-19, when God wants the best for us, he often isolates us and during our isolation we become like the olive. This isolation caused by COVID-19, is new to many but for many of us who are Christians, isolation is not new because as children of God, Proverbs 12:3 reads, "The root of the righteous cannot be moved." We need to be well rooted in our lives by keeping God's truth in the forefront in our lives. Our use of God's Word should be wide-ranging as we apply it to many situations in our life. Reading, understanding, and applying God's Word helps us become rooted in his way, making it difficult for Satan to topple us.

In Matthew 26:36, we read, "Jesus, on this night, was in the garden of Gethsemane". The word Gethsemane is a Greek word that is derived from the Aramaic word

"Gethsemane." It means olive press. This was a garden where olive trees were in abundance and this place was where the olives were pressed.

Proverbs 12:12 tells us that "the root of the righteous yields fruit." Once grounded in God's Word, we should produce fruit in service and love towards others, abundantly like the full harvest of the olive tree. We as children of God in the church are in training, learning to serve, just like a waiter or waitress in a restaurant. These workers make sure that they provide good customer service to ensure that the manager and customers are well pleased, and their needs are met. This takes time and effort, much like the olive tree takes time to produce mature fruit.

For proper fruit development, the olive tree needs pruning. So, it is with us as Christians, whether you are a Pastor, Evangelist, Teacher, Apostle, or whatever office you hold or hold not, pruning is important for everyone to grow. In like manner, God prunes us to produce the best fruit there is. Consider John 15. Christ is the true vine and God the vinedresser. According to verse 2, "Every branch that bears fruit he prunes, that it may bear more fruit." God wants us to have his righteous character. He prunes us accordingly to help us develop as his begotten children.

How does God prune us?

God can prune us in many ways, such as separating us from things that we love and do not want to let go off, separation from people and certain relationships that may be toxic, separation from virus (like the coronavirus). Other ways include separation from food to fasting by allowing you to turn your plates and pots down, prayer, reading the word, praise and worship, teaching us how to be humble, trials and testing, which comes from God but he will also allow the devil to tempt you.

The Holy Spirit is often symbolized as olive oil within the Bible. As first fruits, God has given us access to his Holy Spirit to help us know and understand his way (1

Corinthians 2:12-13). The Holy Spirit will give us strength to overcome our sins and the pressures put upon us by Satan. Our trials can be compared to the pressing or bruising done to the olive to produce the oil. God will allow trials to help us stir up and bring out his Holy Spirit within us. And with use, God will increase our measure of his Holy Spirit much like the oil content increases in the olive as it ripens.

We receive packages and mail from the postman without knowing half of the time what is in them. What this is showing us is that we receive on a day to day basis without even realising it. God wants us to be planted in him for our spiritual gifts to grow, just like the seed and we get to a level of isolation. The seed in the ground is isolated in the soil, mail in the envelope is isolated from the receiver but only exposed, which is elevation once it is open, so is it with our spiritual gifts that god has placed within us and also how we are as Christians in growth.

Jesus makes it crystal clear that prayer shall include both asking in his name, which is known as (Jesus Christ) and receiving that our joy may be full or complete. It is just like a child asking their parents for a present, that they really want and once the parent gives it to them, the child feels complete and full of joy (John 16:24). Again, Jesus said, what things so ever ye desire, when ye pray, believe that ye receive them, and ye shall have them (Mark 11:24). The heart that receives the seed of the word on good ground is one that hears the word, and receives it, and brings forth fruit, some thirtyfold, some sixty, and some a hundred (Mark 4:20). Within churches we often realise that there are some Christians who receive the word of God and accept it gracefully and there are others who are rock stone Christians who hear the word of God and do not receive it, but instead they huff and puff. Even the new birth is not just God giving to us; it is receiving the adoption of sons (Galatians 4:5).

Let us stop working on God for giving unto us and let us allow him to work on us for receiving. When we do not know how to reposition our receiver, the Lord of Glory is more than able to order our steps and direct our hearts in line with the flow of God. Do not abandon your confidence in God. Do not throw away your confidence in God. The Word of God can purge out of us all the leaven of doubt, false teaching, jealousy, envy, past hurt, rejection, lost hope, and more to bring us into the great recompense of a reward in becoming elevated, from great to greater, from disgrace to grace, and from dishonour to honour in the sight of our enemies.

We have need of endurance and a willingness to wait on God because after you have done and fulfilled the will of God, we will see God moving to adjust our position from weakness to strength, obscurity to glory, and isolation to elevation. The Lord knows the right way for us to receive the promise that he has placed upon our life.

Make this your confession now

Although we cannot see everything that our lord and Saviour is doing in our life right now, I know that he is repositioning our receiver because with every passing moment his voice grows clearer. But the path of the just is as the shining light, that shineth more and more unto the perfect day (Proverbs 4:18).

Give God another chance to make it right within your life. When God decides to isolate you, he is doing that to elevate you so that you can be more powerful within him. There is a moment where you realise that God is not done teaching you important lessons. As an adult, you think when you reach a certain age that you already know too much. You have gone through enough experiences in life that have taught you so much about love, heartbreak, wisdom, pain, healing, and starting over. You have met enough people who taught you how to determine who is right or wrong, who is honest and who is shady. Because of this experience, generally, you feel like you have a good sense of judgment when it comes to choosing the people you want in your future and making sensible decisions in your life.

You are aware that life is full of surprises and everything is unpredictable but for some reason, you have faith that what is coming is better than what has passed. You feel like you have learned enough to pass the test and get a good grade, but then something happens that shakes you. Something you did not see coming, something you did not expect, something you thought would never happen to you, and that is the moment you realise that the lessons are not over. That is when you get that you are not prepared for the test and that God is not done teaching you what you need to learn. Therefore, when you have entered his classroom of isolation, you know it is time to learn the steps to your elevation.

You slowly begin to understand that God has denied you certain prayers or certain wishes because his had new lessons, which are going to change your mind or maybe your heart. They will make you wish for different things. They will make you a different person. They will make you thankful that certain things did not work out because they would not have aligned with who you want to become, which Is that powerful member in church who has reached their elevation level in God and not man.

You begin to trust his timing and his plans. It starts making sense when you put two and two together. It adds up. You realise that without these new lessons, you could have made a decision that was going to hurt you or trapped yourself somewhere you do not belong or with someone who makes you miserable. You begin to appreciate the pain, the delays, the setbacks that you faced within your isolation because through them you got to know yourself a little better and have seen the anointing God has placed upon your life. This led you to find yourself and your passion from being at a place of setback (isolation) to a place of comeback (elevation), which makes you a true, rooted, grounded, and mature child a God. These lessons push you to end things and say goodbye to people you loved or wanted to remain in your life. These lessons God has given unto you during your isolation period push you to be in a better place emotionally, mentally, spiritually, physically, or financially.

When God does not give you something you are praying for in your isolation season, it means he is not done teaching you what you need to learn for him to elevate you. He will bring you to and through what will ultimately change you and you will look back and understand why you had to wait in your isolation period for you to begin your elevation season. You will look back and thank him for not granting you those wishes your mind desired.

You will look back and realise that sometimes you wished for things you were not ready for, things you could have easily destroyed if they were yours or even yourself too. You will realize that you still need to learn a few more lessons before you are fully ready to embrace and appreciate his gifts, grace, favour, and his blessings that he has placed upon you when you became elevated. You will realise that you will forever be his student and he will always have the final say as your teacher because you still will not get all the answers right no matter who you are or how much you know. You still need his confirmation. You still need his approval. He is always going to know better. He is always going to prepare you for the hardest tests so you can achieve the greatest score.

God blessed us with the Bible to teach us lessons about how to be the best Christian we can be. God wants us to strive to be as much like Jesus Christ as we possibly can be. He gives us examples in the Bible of how we can live more like him, and we can apply these examples to our day-to-day life. We are not always going to be perfect in living out these lessons, but with practice and consistency we can instil these values into our hearts. The Bible is such a wonderful book and worth studying for a lifetime because we can always grow as people. All we have tried to do is give a big picture of some of the concepts taught over and over in the Bible. Here are five great lessons from the Bible, which is his manual to man on how to be the best Christians we can be.

In the bible, God precisely went looking for Moses. As their leader, Moses himself had to be elevated before he could be commissioned to help Israel become a nation. The Promised Land could never be claimed as an inheritance while the Israelites thought of themselves as slaves. This elevation process began in Genesis 12 when God promised to make Abraham into a great nation and to bless the nations of the world through him. Abraham "broke through" to a level far above the others of his day. By so doing, his descendants were also privileged to enjoy the benefits of that higher level. God wanted to elevate the nation even higher than what Abraham had experienced.

In their first meeting, Abraham was still a stranger in the land. Now, it was time for God to reveal himself as the God of his descendants and for the Promised Land to become their possession. But there was much more!

After entering the Promised Land, the plan was to help them discover an even higher dimension, beyond wealth, lands, and possessions. In that dimension, He could be revealed as "The Lord God Jehovah," their true inheritance. The God of Glory wanted a personal relationship with all of Israel and to become their personal treasure with limitless value.

Therefore, the tribe of Levi was forbidden to inherit property in the Promised Land. God would be their inheritance. This was meant to be a prophetic model of how God would become every citizen's treasure in the nation of Israel because he was a worshipper. God revealed a beautiful concept through David. Though he was not of the tribe of Levi, David broke through.

Are you noticing changes within your mind, body, soul, and spirit? If you have begun a journey towards a higher level of consciousness, there will be both mental and physical changes that accompany you on your path as your mindset will be much different to what it was before.

Things that you never thought were possible will suddenly be revealed to you. Higher levels of consciousness enable higher levels of understanding, and with this shift comes many changes. As you begin your journey, you will look at the world differently. You will experience a shift in your spiritual belief system that will alter your core beliefs.

If you are experiencing any of the following signs, you are likely shifting to that higher level of consciousness. Embrace the change and enjoy the ride.

As God shifts you into a higher level of your conscious mind, you can let go of all the aggression and anger you once clung to. You have no room for all the noise that is created by feelings of ill will as you are completely focused on your own inner workings. You simply do not have the time for hostility in any form.

You take full responsibility for your life and where you are right now

You know that your past is a result of your reactions to experiences today, and you must stop blaming others for your mistakes that YOU chose to make. You realize that you must not only embrace the past, but you also must learn from it. If you do not effectively close the door on the past, it will drag you down in the future. Through meditation and self-reflection, you now own every aspect of your life. You give the reins to no one.

You own your emotions

You know that if you want to be happy and successful in life, it must come from within your soul. You are completely capable of creating the life that you want to live, and you make affirming choices to move yourself in that direction. You should no longer rely on others to bring you happiness. You can now slow down and spend quiet time with yourself without feeling as if you are not being productive. You are no longer afraid of what might happen in life because you are prepared for any obstacle that may come your way.

You practice self-love

You should take care of your own needs before addressing the needs of others because you will be better prepared in helping others in areas of their life if you address the need for help with areas in yours. You know that you will only be able to care for others when you are well cared for yourself. You no longer expect perfection from yourself. Instead, you embrace the imperfections and celebrate them and slowly improve them. You see them as what they really are: opportunities to learn and grow into higher levels of consciousness and elevation. You have a strong desire to be alone, so that you can continue to explore the inner workings of your mind.

You are kind, loving, and compassionate

You forgive yourself and others for past hurt. You enjoy helping others on their Christian journeys. You are forever purifying yourself and asking yourself day in and out about what you can do for those around you. People have become attracted to your kind energy, and you notice them wanting to spend time with you.

Something strong inside of you is motivating you to make significant changes in your life. That something inside of you might be activated because of the Holy Ghost, which occurs when you are in your isolation period and you learn to become closer with God. Your gut tells you that it is time to take a leap of faith and make changes happen within your life. As you begin to shift to a higher level of consciousness, there are several things that no longer fit. You have realized that you should only be spending your time and energy on the things in life that directly matter and fulfil your newly found purpose that will take you to your God ordained destiny. Your job, your home, and your personal belongings may be pulled into question as you shift to a higher awareness when you have reached that level of elevation.

You pull away from toxic people

You no longer tolerate those that suck your positive energy. Drama does not appeal to you, and you want no part of it in your life. While it is not easy, you find yourself ending friendships and setting boundaries that you have never set before. Toxic energy will only slow down your transition, and you know that you only have room in your life for those that have your best interests at heart.

You have trouble sleeping

Often as people transition to a higher level of a conscious state, they have trouble staying asleep at night. Do not be alarmed if this happens to you on your journey of isolation to elevation. Your subconscious mind is hard at work thinking, which becomes a normal thing for you and there may be times during the night hours that it needs to send a message to your conscious mind.

You get rid of all your destructive habits

If you used to eat unhealthy foods, drink alcohol, spend a lot of time on social media, sleeping or smoking, do not be surprised if you no longer want to engage in any of those old, dirty bad habits. Now that your knowledge and eyes are open, you are beginning to see the long-term success entailed in giving up short term fulfilments. Now that you understand and truly embrace this ideology, you can simply leave the bad habits behind.

God wants to teach us:

- **Love others**

Many of us turn to Corinthians 13 to learn the definition of love. God wants us to understand what real love means and what it entails (that it is kind, patient, and trusts).

- **Be humble**

God wants us to be humble, and he shares this in 2 Chronicles 7:14, which says "If my people, who are called by my name, will humble themselves, and pray and seek my face and turn from their wicked ways, then I will hear from heaven, and I will forgive their sin and will heal their land." God tells us that when we put aside our ego and ask for forgiveness of our sins during our isolation, that we can get the most beautiful blessing of heaven, which is elevation.

- **Do the right thing**

Doing the right thing is not always easy. In many instances what is right does not always appear as a black and white situation. The life of Joseph, in Genesis chapters 37-50 have a lot of examples of how doing the right thing can be difficult. He had his share of complicated situations and hard times to deal with, but he was guided by God. He chose to obey God's instructions and do right by others around him, which led to his favour with God. When we are faced with a difficult situation, we can turn to God and ask for his help. Pray to him and consult with the Bible and learn the right thing to do without difficulty. The way in which he teaches us to do the right thing is by bringing us through an isolation period to become elevated.

- **Manage conflict with respect**

Respecting others can be hard at times, and God understands that we will make mistakes. When people are rude to us, it can be hard not to respond with anger. The Bible teaches us to live peaceably with those around us (Romans 12:18, 19). We are taught the Golden Rule from childhood: treat others the way you want to be treated.

- **Do not worry what people think of you**

All of God's children need to stop worrying about what other people think of them. Living a life in envy of others and thinking that they are better than you are, is only going to destroy your self-esteem and hence why

God allows you to be tested through your isolation to get your elevation. Instead, we only need to care more about what God thinks of you than what man, pastors, teachers, friends, family, or even sinners think of you. In the end, I will not be judged by how I measured up according to their standards or where I stood with them but how I measure by Christ's standards and where I stood with him. If I have God's approval, I do not need to waste time thinking about how I may get everyone else's because it does not really matter once God has taken me to the level of isolation.

God teaches us lessons on how to be better people. He wants to instil in us the values and morals of a good human being so that we can become more like Jesus Christ. We should work every day to live out these lessons in every interaction. That is why he teaches us everything we need to know through our isolation period so we can be elevated in him then we will be able to pass these lessons on to our children, family, or friends. By doing so, the level of anointing that is upon our lives once we get to the place of isolation shall help the world grow to be a better place.

I put it for your consideration that when you have been isolated you have a laser-like focus on your goals, so you can get more work done. You work more efficiently because you are more present in everything you do. No longer do you submit yourself to distractions and all that is going on around you. Your priorities are pure (perhaps thanks to a vision board). For the bible says in (Habakkuk 2:2-3), "And the Lord answered me, and said, write the vision, and make it plain upon tables, that he may run that readeth it. For the vision is yet for an appointed time, but at the end it shall speak, and not lie though it tarry, wait for it; because it will surely come, it will not tarry " And you do not waste any time in what you are doing for God. You are doing what needs to be done to achieve your dreams. Your stress levels are down, too, because you have a sense of the bigger picture, and you can see how it all fits together.

You no longer feel the need to compete. You end up forgetting the reason why you always felt the need to prove yourself before towards people such as family, friends or even church members. You no longer need to compete with everyone because you no longer compare yourself to others as you know that Jesus Christ is on your side. You now know that by helping others instead of competing with them, you are helping yourself to improve your future.

You have a vast sense of gratitude. You appreciate all you have within your life and all the things you will have in the future because God's word says in Psalm 34:8, "O taste and see that the Lord is good: blessed is the man that trusteth in him." Gratitude is part of your daily quiet time. You see all the good in the world, and you are grateful for it. You are grateful for love, peace, joy, and happiness within the world. While you know that there is much work to do, you are grateful that you can be a part of the solution instead of the problem.

As you shift to a higher level of dimension consciousness, you will realize your entire life begins to change. You think back to the person that you used to be. You think back to the one who was lying, stealing, committing adultery, or fornicating whatever it may be. You realize how immature and selfish you were compared to the person you are today. You have made significant changes, and you will forever have more power than the person you once were because God is in control of your life .

You need to embrace the changes that God has put in your life as it will bring you a higher level of satisfaction in your own life, as well as an innate ability to help others. These changes are a good because they mean you are shifting into something better than before. Make peace with everyone knowing that the changes are leading you to a more fulfilling life with God. You are becoming the amazing person that you were born to be. **"But seek ye first the kingdom of God, and his** righteousness; and all these things shall be added unto you" (Matthew 6:33).

Chapter 7

I slipped
through the gaps

Have you ever just missed the school bell when the teacher was just about to close the door and you slipped through hiding in the bundle of the other students with the teacher unaware you slipped in? So often we slip through the gap in life but thankfully God is there to put us back together and close that gap for us.

"Then they took up stones to cast at him. My Jesus hid himself. And went out of the temple. Going to the midst of them" (John 8:59).

And he passed by, they picked up stones to kill Jesus, this is happening there while he is almost at church. Jesus is God who was in church. So, Jesus got to hide in church from saints trying to kill him. And he slipped out before a benediction.

I want to teach you all today using as a subject, *I slipped through the gaps.*

I slipped through the gaps, look at your neighbour and say pray for me. Look at them and say I know you cannot tell but I slipped through the cracks. As Christians called to preach, we must ensure that we look and find something that is unfamiliar within a familiar passage and then raise questions that the congregation will not know how to ask about. In so doing, I thought about Genesis chapter 3.

In Genesis chapter 3, we are mindful of wind. The serpent had come into the beautiful garden of Eden that was once paradise to man. The serpent seduced Eve to eat of the forbidden fruit. And the layout of the text gives us the insight and knowledge to know that the tree of knowledge was positioned in the centre of the garden. Using deductive reasoning, we understand that on that day Eve, which was made from Adams ribs, was there giving direction as to where the tree stands. While they are having the conversation, at this point they are not standing next to the tree and so in order for them to get to the tree of knowledge that held the forbidden fruit, they need to go through the entire orchard. While walking throughout the entire orchard, they had passed by trees and they passed by many fruits that they could have chosen and eaten. I want to exegete. The trees that were passed were amazing and it was extraordinary that those trees were growing fresh fruits. From a contemporary standard version, they say that the fruit tree was flush with fresh apples as it was in the place of paradise. They were not from different seasons but rather it was just from one season. So, can you imagine what could have been going on or going through the mind of the fruits of the trees that were being passed, to get to the tree and the fruits that they should not have. The trees within the garden had on them whispering leaves, which kept on asking the thoughtful question. They ask other question such as: Why have you not chosen to pick me? I know that I have what you need and lack within yourself. I will be able to provide unto your strength. I will equip you for your journey but regardless you still walk past and overlook me. Whatever you do please do not look quickly at the people who are on your row. Because some of them throbbing in the back of their mind are asking the question. How come I was not picked. How come I was not chosen? How come I was not selected? How come I was overlooked? And somehow in your sub-conscious, you have been stained with low self-esteem. Over the rejection of not being selected.

Before those fruit had fallen from the tree, they had to have conclude at some point, I am glad that I was not picked. We need to understand this, that you were not picked because you are not Satan's taste or his type. If he had chosen you, then you would have been the form of evidence that is what he liked. Saints, we need to give God glory that you were never chosen because if you had been picked it would have caused you too much stress. There has been to many years of your life and too much anxiety in our lives were we only know how to shout for what we are chosen for but sometimes you have got to give God glory for what you were ignored about. Children of God, thank God for the job that you did not get. Thank God for the psychopath, stalker, or deceiver that you did not marry. Thank God for the house that you never moved into. Thank god for the option you never chose. Today, children of God, you have got to be at peace for slipping in through the gaps. You did not see it then, but you see it now. Would you just stop for a moment and give God a shout of praise for what you were not chosen?

Earlier in this year, on a Wednesday night, which was supposed to be their practice night as they have choir rehearsal every Wednesday, but on this particular

Wednesday in March of this year, no one arrived on time. Every single member of the gospel choir of West Side Baptist Church in Beatrice, Nebraska was late. Can you imagine that? They had no idea what was taking place. However, choir practice was supposed to start at 7, yet nobody showed up on time. Then at 7:20, there is an explosion due to a gas leak in the building. The explosion took off the roof and blew off the steeple. The blast decimated the sanctuary. Hymnals were found 500 feet away. Yet, all the choir were tardy for different reasons.

The pianist and her mother, the choir director, were pulled over for speeding tickets. Sisters Lucille and Dorothy were captivated watching the Marpo Live show The ST brother's car would not start. They were waiting on triple A to give them a jump to their battery. Donna Vanderbilt, a high school sophomore, was grounded and could not go to choir rehearsal because she had not finished her geometry homework. Harvey Brown lost track of time talking to his next-door neighbour. The pastor, who lit the furnace in the first place, was late because he was ironing his daughter's dress as his wife was out of town.

I am here for 50 of you who do not even realize you thought you were running late. But you are right on schedule. God was blocking you from something you did not even see. I do not know who is going to receive this prophetic word as I know you been watching other people go ahead of you, but you forgot God always saves the best for last. And for 15 of you all that shout today, God said, watch what I do for the last 6 weeks of the year. I am getting ready to bless you with what eyes have not seen and ears have not heard. You are getting ready to catch up with the blessing you thought you lost.

In 1988, Pseudo was on his way home back to New York after attending a wedding in England. He had checked in his luggage and then went into the airport lounge to relax because he had enough time to spare. He had a couple of drinks ad before he knew it, the intercom announced that the gate was closing for the flight to take off. He gathered himself and headed down to the counter but the Pan Am flight ticket agent refused to let him on the plane at all. He was too drunk to discuss it, so he went back to sleep right on the bench inside the airport where the gate was. Unbeknownst to the him, he had missed the Pan Am flight 103, which would become known as the Lockerbie bombing. The explosion killed every person on the plane except for one that was left on the ground. He was isolated and maybe even felt unfairly treated from the others on the flight and unknown slipped through the gaps because of the brokenness, which was upon his life. It was being that drunk that had been the cause of him missing his flight. Some of us should be giving God glory that we have the grace of God upon our life when we did not even know it was there. When I was out of order, grace was still with me. When I was doing stuff, I had no business doing, the hand of God was still on my life and I slipped through the gaps. Immediately, in a person's life, there are instances when slipping through the gaps can mean the difference between life or death, from isolation to elevation.

This message is not for spectators nor criticizers. This message is a word of encouragement for those who call themselves Christians or a child of God who reads this book for a fresh fire and who are seeking to step out of their isolation season into their elevation purpose. They have a dance, shout, and praise in their spirit. God said, while you praise me in this season today, whatever plans the enemy has waiting to do in your house, in your life, or even in your time of isolation is now disrupted. Every level of spiritual warfare aimed at your house is being brought down while you shout praises unto God. If you do not have a shout, the enemy is waiting on you. But if you have a clap in your hands and a Halleluiah shout in your mouth, God said I am getting ready to disregard every weapon every worker of iniquity that is on your family and your household, shall be covered under the blood of Jesus because you are moved from a place of isolation into a location of elevation.

Often, as Christians we need correction from God, not approval of our own or other actions, which are not of him and his will for our life. I just want the message of this book to reach as many people as possible so that you do not to fall through the gaps and you get to the level of elevation where God has designed you to be.

I feel glory coming out, your children should be the head and not the tail, your children shall prophecy. Thank you, God, I just cleared for take-off when you speak you children's name out loud, they are getting out of jail early and they already have a scholarship.

In John chapter 8:12-20, they argue over his testimony "Then spake Jesus again unto them, saying, I am the light of the world: he that followeth me shall not walk in darkness, but shall have the light of life. The Pharisees therefore said unto him, thou bearest record of thyself; thy record is not true. Jesus answered and said unto them, Though I bear record of myself, yet my record is true: for I know whence I came, and whither I go; but ye cannot tell whence I come, and whither I go.

Ye judge after the flesh; I judge no man. And yet if I judge, my judgment is true: for I am not alone, but I and the Father that sent me. It is also written in your law, that the testimony of two men is true. I am one that bear witness of myself, and the Father that sent me beareth witness of me. Then said they unto him, where is thy Father? Jesus answered, Ye neither know me, nor my Father: if ye had known me, ye should have known my Father also. These words spake Jesus in the treasury, as he taught in the temple: and no man laid hands on him; for his hour was not yet come".

They argue with the master because he said I am the light of the world. Whoever follows me will never walk in darkness. But will have the light of life. The Pharisees push back and say it appears you are your own witness. There is no greater freedom than not needing anybody for anything. Some of you reading this book have been delivered from drugs. Some of the persons reading this book have been delivered from alcohol. There are people within both the world and church, some of you reading this book have been delivered from pornography or some of you may have been delivered from gambling, stealing, jealousy, envy, sabotaging, bad mind, or lying. There are those of you that have been delivered even from other people's opinions.

It says in john 8:21-27, the dispute is over who Jesus is. Jesus had finally come to the decision that that I do not need to defend myself because I am tired of having to dumb myself down for those people who are insecure or who are threatened about who and what I represent. Saints of God, we need to understand that if it had not been for the Lord on my side during my isolation where would I have been? I went through too much stuff in my life to have to worry about what others think about me. Where were you when they cut off my lights? Where were you when I had no job? Where were you when I was raised my child with no child support? Where were you when I had no food to eat? Where were you when I had sleepless nights because of the enemies? Some of you, I need you to know you are not on trial. Stop defending yourself because you are not on trial. Stop defending yourself, you are found guilty for having faith and favour within God that has moved you from a place of isolation. The favour of God is undeniably on your life and your haters cannot stand it because God has moved you into your elevation season. What you have received, you did not have to sleep with anybody to get it, you did not have to compromise to get it. Because God is the joy and strength of your life and with joy you were able to draw water from the well of salvation.

Joy, Joy, Joy in the Lord. Do not let anybody steal your joy. Joy in the Lord.

In John chapter 8, as we come now to the edge of the text, verse 48 says, that they got mad because Jesus starts talking about eternal life and they said how did people and even Abraham have to die, and he is the father of our faith. Have we moved it to such a season in our faith that we no longer preach eternal life? Are we only preaching to a shallow Christianity about how they are wrapped around entrepreneurship and what it is that you can gain but we no longer talk about sacrifice, that if you suffer with him then you will rein with him? He understood that this world is not my home, YET WILL I TRUST HIM.

Some of you cannot give a shout of praise or thanksgiving to show your gratitude and honour because you have never been sick before. But for those of us who know what sickness feels like, you can reckon with a glorious power packed Holy Ghost shout of praise saying he was wounded for your transgressions and bruised for your iniquity and by his stripes, we are healed. They got mad because they were wondering how he was operating with this level of authority. They were trying to figure out how was he able to gauge that depth of their Revelation and he was not a part of their fellowship.

I have had some good days, I have had some bad days, but I will not complain. I have a job that I do not qualify for. So, here Jesus is in church and while he was in church, he discovers what many of you have found out and that is just because people go to church does not mean they want the best for you. Just because you are in church does not mean everybody gets excited about your blessing. People are disappointed about the doors that you have opened. They picked up stones to kill Jesus. In the Text it says that he is in church. The critical question that I must ask is why they would be bringing weapons to church. God help me.

Maybe you forgot, I am in John chapter 8, and the narrative is where the woman is caught in adultery. And Jesus said to that whole body, he that is without sin in him cast the first stone. They threw down their stone according to John chapter 8, but by the time I get the verse 48, it is evident they pick the stone back up. There are some people who been waiting for an opportunity for you to be killed. They are waiting for the moment for you to fall, they are waiting for an opportunity to blow up your spot. But they do not know it is too late. If you were going to kill me, you should have got to me before I became elevated by God. But the moment I get isolated, what the enemy thought he was going to do to me, it has been disconnected. I slipped through the gaps once again. Some of you just made it through without any provocation, distraction, or annoyance but there are a few of you in the body of Christ that can identify and testify with the message that I'm trying to share with you, which is that you know you made it by the hair on your chinny chin, by the grace of God. God help me to write this right. If a person is beside you while reading this book tell them, I slipped through the gaps. I have slipped through the gaps; the Devil has lost again.

They think they are going to kill Jesus in church. But they do not understand that you can never wound a worshipper. If you were going to get me you should have got me before I got here that is why real worshippers do not sit still, because they know that there is a contract out on their life and as long as you keep moving God will move with you. God said, if you give me glory today and do not sit still, whatever attack that had been aimed at your life, you are going to escape every attack that the enemy throws at you. You slipped through the gaps. Give God praise that it is over, give God glory that it is over, because you slipped through the gaps and have made it out from isolation to elevation.

REMINDER FOR YOU!

He saw the best in you when everyone else around saw the worst in you.

He saw that you were destined for power, purpose, breakthrough, double portion or anointing and deliverance.

You must go through your isolation period to come out elevated with Christ to slay your giants against your destiny and the pharaohs against your purpose.

From great to greater, from weakness to strength, from lo-da-ba to the kings table and from isolation to elevation.

I AM ELEVATED IN CHRIST JESUS.

I am honoured and blessed that God as chosen to separate me. Separation brings revelation and revelation brings elevation. If you are asking what I just said, separation brings revelation and revelation brings elevation when God separates you from things, places, and persons. He is doing so for a reason because he wants to bring you into a place where he can teach you more about himself and develop a more intimate relationship with and in him. Through that process he will teach you about the Holy Spirit, Angelic realm, and demonic spirits. He will teach you about faith, discerning of spirits for you to identify what spirit is in operation, human spirts, word of wisdom, train you in your authority, how you can worship in truth. He will train you to see in the realm of the spirit, and spiritual warfare. God will teach you secret things and how he should entrust you in and how to understand your blessing, or even take you to a place of word of knowledge this is something that is supernatural, not what could be attained through natural means.

Daniel chapter 3, (this still manages to shock me about the cost of a fire), "Then the princes, the governors, and captains, the judges, the treasurers, the counsellors, the sheriffs, and all the rulers of the provinces, were gathered together unto the dedication of the image that Nebuchadnezzar the king had set up; and they stood before the image that Nebuchadnezzar had set up."

Shadrach, Meshach and Abed-nego was cast into the fiery furnace from the illustration shown within the bible we can understand that not a hair on their heads was changed. Their clothing was not scorched, and they never got burned. This is to show that by maintaining to live a life of faith, they did not give in to the king's threat because they knew that God would deliver them out of it. When you live a life of faith, you can make the following declaration, I have been through hell, but I still smell like heaven. I want you to speak it into the atmosphere so that the devil can hear you say, I have been through hell, but I still smell like heaven. I have been through isolation, but I still smell like elevation.

Say to the one who cannot tolerate you or celebrate you, I went through my isolation and now I am clothed in my elevation. I have been in the fires of hell, but I still smell like heaven. Tell it to those who have ears to hear it, I have been through the heat, but I have not been scorched despite the heat was hot as hell, I still smell like heaven. When faith goes to the fire, this will transport favour from this message to every reader of this book.

The situation in the narrative of Daniel chapter 3, I am compelled to issue a disclaimer due to the very fact that if you have never been through anything at all, the devil has never risen to shut you down. If you have never experienced a proverbial fire, the figurative of this message may very well not be for you. You may be motivated to check the latest post on Facebook page, Instagram, Twitter, or WhatsApp. But if you like faith of the Hebrew boys in Daniel 3, you are going to the furnace right now. The devil is trying to rob you of your faith and trying to destroy your destiny and the word God has spoken over your life. It feels like you are in hell and you feel like it is the end and you cannot take anymore but God is saying through his revelation, you have been through hell, but you still smell like heaven.

- ✓ Separation brings isolation

- ✓ Isolation bring revelation

- ✓ Revelation brings elevation

Saint of God, no matter what you have been through it may be rough, it may be tough, it may be hot like the fiery furnace, but once God is with you and you carry the mark of Jesus on you, you may not look like what you have been through. Separation did not break you; Isolation did not kill you, revelation built you, and elevation lifted you to a place of promotion and not demotion. You will be smiling at your neighbours, your haters and your celebrators and say but God, but God, but God, but God. Only God can do it. If he has done it for me, he can do it for you.

Because the promises of god are still yea and Amen. You will come out and this is prophetic not pathetic.

You will come out smelling like heaven and not the hell you have been through. You will come out looking like elevation with all your revelation despite being separated due to isolation. You will come out smelling like heaven when you refuse to worship the God of Babylon. When you are a true child of God you will not settle for less than what God has for you. People of all races, verse 4-5 of Daniel 3 says, "Then a herald cried aloud, To you it is commanded, O people, nations, and languages, That at what time ye hear the sound of the cornet, flute, harp, sackbut, psaltery, dulcimer, and all kinds of music, ye fall down and worship the golden image that Nebuchadnezzar the king hath set up."

Nations and languages, listen to the King Nebuchadnezzar when you hear the sound of the music out of the ground, bow and worship King Nebuchadnezzar's gold statues and anyone who refused to obey would immediately be thrown into a blazing furnace. We are the Joshua generation, a prophetic minority living in a perfect world. This is the new chapter of spiritual and moral Babylonian captivity. We cannot deny the fact that the spirit of Nebuchadnezzar is alive and well. And now I can say that the devil wants us to worship him and to bow down. It has always been about bowing down. Matthew chapter 4:9 states it has an encounter with Jesus in the wilderness where the devil wanted Jesus to bow down and worship him. The enemy wants you to bow, to kneel, to surrender while he makes war and conflict against you.

Be reminded that today's complacency is tomorrow's captivity. Always remember we are what we tolerate. Within this world there are things that we have tolerated in this generation, that we should have reviewed. Always remember, that instead of being so focused on waiting for Jesus to come, that Jesus is waiting for us to stand up for his name's sake at this moment in time. It is simple. God does not want us to settle for less than what he has for us, but the enemy wants you to settle for less and become limited.

If you can settle for that golden statue of Nebuchadnezzar, you can settle for less. You can settle for the things the devil has to offer and therefore, you are a sell out against God just like Judas, one of Jesus's disciples who sold him to the enemy for 30 pieces of silver. Do not settle for a statue made of gold, when you know you serve a mighty God who is filled with grace. There is milk and honey waiting for you in the promise land.

You know that you are more than a conqueror when Jesus was resurrected, so God was drawing you when he made you according to the model, he has visions for you. Turn to your neighbour and say do not settle for less than what God has to offer you. And by the way the scriptural nation that the enemy would attempt to offer you is nothing but a contradiction. Sometimes the enemy will offer you something less than what God really holds for you. Nebuchadnezzar always wanted just one thing. He always wanted the people of God to worship the false God, to sacrifice the truth, and to rewrite the Bible, which is politically culturally incorrect.

I am here sitting at the computer writing this message so that we can see and identify that we are just like the Hebrew boys in Daniel chapter 3, in the name of Jesus. We are just like them to decree and declare that we are children of God, who know our authorities and are not afraid to let the devil know we are warriors and soldiers. We are not afraid get in trouble, so we are here to declare into the decree in the name of Jesus that there is a new Joshua generation that will not be intimidated. We will not bow down. We will not surrender because we live a life of faith. We live a life of faith.

You will come out smelling like heaven even though you have been through hell. For those of us who have been in isolation with God, we know whose we are and to whom we belong and so therefore we refuse to bow to the enemy. We know that we have to bow to God for in Philippians 2:10-11 it says, "That at the name of Jesus every knee should bow, of things in heaven, and things in earth, and things under the earth; And that every tongue should confess that Jesus Christ is Lord, to the glory of God the Father."

We are not going to bow to any idols or other false Gods, in the name of Jesus. The day is coming where knees from different cultures and countries must bow at the name of Jesus to Jesus. Some new, some old, some fat, some skinny, some brown, some black, some white, some hard, or soft. The day is coming!

Quickly, you will come out smelling like heaven when you declare that Jesus Christ is Lord.

I just want to let somebody know that at some point you cannot embrace what God has for you until you first accept what God did for you. This is just like with your time in isolation, you must go through your period of isolation to receive your elevation. One of the most powerful declarations is to declare you know the story, we do not need to defend ourselves because we know that the God we serve is able to defend us but if not, we still will not bow to any Idols or false Gods. Let us make a powerful declaration that God is able, Jesus Christ is able, and I believe that God is able.

We have faith and the confidence from Heaven, where we have the assurance that things that we cannot see actually took place within the spiritual realm before it manifested into the natural.

Christian are either people of faith or people of little faith. **"Christ is the author and the finisher of our faith" (Hebrews 12:2).**

"We've all been given that measure of faith" (Romans 12:3).

"So, faith cometh by hearing, and hearing by the word of God" (Romans 10:17).

Having little faith is what caused Cain to give God the second-best offering. Little faith looks back instead of looking forward. Remember Lot's wife. Instead of speaking with Moses, the people of Israel began to murmur and complain about not having enough food to last them for another day, they were people of little faith. Peter was walking on the water and took his eyes off Jesus because he had little faith.

Every single time in the gospel we see the connection supporting what the Hebrew boys declared in the company of God, which is that through their faith God is able. We know that God is able, when we look throughout the Bible, we see that God is able. He was able to die that our sins may be forgiven, he was able to rise, and conquered the devil, death, hell, and the grave.

"And the living one. I died, and behold I am alive forevermore, and I have the keys of Death and Hades" (Revelation 1:18).

What you have been asking for it shall come to pass; your season of isolation is over because God has elevated you and the best is yet to come.

Joseph's brothers placed him in a pit and then they sold him into Egypt and after that he become prime minister to that country.

When you are a child of God and God wants to rise you up to another level of promotion in him, then all kinds of situation and adversary from the enemy will show up. The more you get to understand God, the more pressure, stress, and depression will present. So, you can rest assured in knowing that your isolation is a pit that will bring you into elevation.

Remember. that going through pain will bring you gain. The same God who allowed you to be in the isolation will take you out of your isolation to a place of elevation.

Remember, Joseph! God took him from a pit to be a prime minister. God will take you from the pit to the pulpit. God will make you a messenger and give you message.

In isolation you will come up against pharaoh, but pharaoh will have to let you go when God speaks on your behalf.

Even in isolation God has given you power over every power of the enemy. Even though you are going through your isolation the enemy will see you and cannot touch you or defeat you.

Whenever a person is set apart or in separation, they will seek to receive revelation for things to be revealed to them concerning their lives past, present, or future. Of where they are coming from and where they are at this present moment and where they will be in the future. So, they want to identify where they can establish their present position to be able to move forward in their future potential in God. In the revelation that will give them insight to being elevated in new dimensions for the things of God and his glory.

For the Bible says, deep calleth unto deep (Psalm 42:7). And to know the deep things of God, you have got to be separated to be motivated to receive revelation through meditation in reaching your God given potential in elevation. As a child of God, when you receive revelation, that means something that was there in the supernatural suddenly will appear in the natural. Meditation is what brings revelation. In meditating you have to be focused and concentrating to think upon God and what he is revealing to you while waiting in silence to hear from God as he speaks from a place of meditation (Joshua 1:8).

"Now unto him who can keep you from falling, and to present you faultless before the presence of his glory with exceeding joy" (Jude 1:24).

I would identify people in isolation as "all alone", "lone ranger", or "isolated". You may have felt like you could not be a part of a community or church organisation. Despite you knowing the importance church had on believers, God had put you in that position of isolation where you were isolated from among many. You were not finding yourself doing what other saints were doing simply because of what God wanted you to do, which was to be isolated knowing that it would elevate you in the near future. People thought that you acting a certain way meant that you thought you were better than them, not knowing that God was purposely making you act that way in order for you to draw yourself away from others. God was also allowing the devil to tempt you while you were in your isolation period because God and the devil knows that we were more vulnerable to Satan's attacks. 1 Peter 5:8 says, "Be sober-minded; be watchful. Your adversary the devil prowls around like a roaring lion, seeking someone to devour." The enemy is a coward, so he plays dirty, and usually chooses to target those who have been put into isolation by God as they are weak and defenceless without fellowship. He knows he is not powerful enough to go after those who are united in fellowship because, "Though one may be overpowered, two can defend themselves. A cord of three strands is not quickly broken" (Ecclesiastes 4:12). That is why it is so important to be rooted in the Body of Christ. And the only way to do that is to surround ourselves with like-minded Christians.

I do not have much in the way of physical family. Many of my family members died when I was young, and a few more have died through the years. But God has placed my lonely heart in a spiritual family, my church, King Jesus Pentecostal Fellowship, and it changed my life. It kept me from isolating myself without God's approval and becoming more depressed. And although it did not happen overnight, I slowly found the strength to move on past my hurt with love and I am here to tell you so can you, too. Whenever you feel the desire to isolate, which is not a will of God, fight it! In fact, push harder to get out and do things with other people. Take your kids to the park or mall, even when you do not feel like it and bring a friend along too. Invite a friend over to dinner, even when you are not in the best of moods. Get out and serve at a local homeless shelters or food banks and invite your Bible study group to come along.

There are many ways to occupy yourself and involve others while doing so. Not only will it be beneficial to you but to others as well. It will keep you from slipping into a dangerous depression, oppression, or suppression but you may just make some new friends during what the darkest days of your life could have been.

This is the air I breathe. From the moment I have reached my elevation, his presence in the power of the Holy Ghost is inside of me. When you can breathe and truly feel the life of God inside of you, it is a mighty encounter and I am going to enjoy every impartation that he gives me.

My cry today is, God I belong to you and only you. Saints, wherever you are shout a praise unto God letting him know that you are ever so appreciative and thankful for everything he has done in our lives.

 Sometimes within church, we hear people talking about backsliders and those who do not go to church anymore as if they are one and the same. (I use the term "church" in its generally accepted modern sense of a building where people gather for religious reasons. This may include the true Church plus any other religious minded person.)

A Christian who has stopped going to church is not necessarily backslidden, but even a backslider needs to be pitied rather than condemned. A backslidden person may fall into two groups. The first group would include a person who goes to church yet has never been born again, which means being baptised in Jesus name. They may have enjoyed the social life of the church but have now gone back into the world or have one foot in the world while still attending lukewarm church meetings. The other, is someone who was at one time saved but for whatever reasons has now gone back into the world. I pray that these shall eventually, like the prodigal son, return. We cannot see a person's heart, so only God knows those who are part of his family, and those who never knew Him.

To the person who is privileged to be in fellowship and who has never experienced being isolated before, it may seem likely that someone who no longer goes to church must be a backslidden or a disobedient Christian. This presumption brings undeserved condemnation on the

Christian who is longing for true, scriptural, fellowship yet finds it difficult to find any, plus there is the added hurt of being misunderstood. Many Christians today are bruised stems or burning flax, they do not need breaking or snuffing out but rather understanding, love, and encouragement.

Each individual case must be taken on its own merit. When someone is out of fellowship, it does not automatically follow, they are backslidden, as some would imply. This is possible of course, but we cannot jump to that conclusion. What about those who God has caused to be isolated while he works in their life? I am thinking of the Apostle Paul. After becoming a Christian, he went into Arabia and conferred not with flesh and blood so that he might learn of God (Galatians 1 v 16-17).

Also, of course there is the Apostle John who was exiled to the Isle of Patmos.

Do you not think it possible that for a time God may take Christians today into a place of isolation while he works in their life? It is not only possible that God is working in their lives but also possible they have a closer walk with the Lord than many Christians who 'go to church'.

Should one go to an apostate church or one that is dead in religion if they cannot find any other in their vicinity? Man might think so, but God says, "Come out of her my people" (Revelation 18:4). God's people are called without the camp, bearing his reproach (Hebrews 13:13).

What did Jesus have to say about the missing sheep? He says that if one sheep out of a hundred is lost, the shepherd leaves the 99 and goes into the mountain to look for the one who is lost (Matthew 18:12-13). There could be many reasons why the sheep is not with the other 99.

Of course, there are many people today who are out of fellowship because the churches they have belonged to are now teaching false doctrine (or no doctrine). They long for fellowship but they do not know where to go. They try different churches and yet like Jesus they find "nowhere to lay their head" (Matthew 8:20). They are out of fellowship. Are they also backslidden?

If a person is backslidden, they simply have turned their backs on worshipping and serving God and going back out into the world or they have turned back to worshipping false gods. They have forsaken their first love and fallen into error and the wrong doctrine. A backslidden person might be quite at home at their local church on Sunday, while another person who walks close to God might find themselves, for a time, in isolation and soon realise that being in isolation leads to elevation.

In the last days there will be a great falling away, but it will not be a falling away from church attendance but rather a falling away from true doctrine. The church buildings might be full of people all having a great time with their professional groups playing their worldly music. It would seem obvious to all and sundry that there is something wrong with that miserable Christian who refuses to join them and ends up going nowhere. However, that miserable Christian may be the only one holding onto true doctrine.

While waiting in your isolation period as a child of God there are certain keys and principles one has to ensure that they take with them; the same way that when you are sick you choose to take certain medication from your doctor to help with the sickness. This is the same that we as children of God need to ensure that we take certain pills that are prescribed for us from God through the Holy Ghost. And these are keys to ensure you take these tablets daily as required while you are in your isolation waiting to go through the door of your elevation and transformation.

Just know that the lord thy God will sustain you, look not to the left or to the right, nor to weak or strong, but be he steadfast in prayer and fasting reverencing that which is a holy time for your transformation and remember to be still in peace and that God loves you always.

- ✓ Pill of patients
- ✓ Pill of hope
- ✓ Pill of joy
- ✓ Pill of peace
- ✓ Pill of courage
- ✓ Pill of passion
- ✓ Pill of penitent

And most of all, pill of grace and favour from God.

Father, I thank you for the promotion that comes through you in my time of isolation to elevation in Jesus name.

Father reject every form of backwardness in my life, in the name of Jesus elevation, elevation, elevation.

I paralyse every strongman assigned to my life and destiny because I must reach my place of elevation in the name of Jesus.

Let every agent of stagnation and delays due to setbacks from trials of isolation working against me be paralysed, in the name of Jesus.

I paralyse the activities of household wickedness over my elevation, in the name of Jesus.

I quench every strange fire from witches and wizards against me in the mighty and powerful name of Jesus.

Lord, endow me with power to maximize my potentials, in the name of Jesus I shall elevate, I must elevate, I will elevate, Amen.

O Lord give me the grace to achieve effortless results by your grace in my time of isolation.

Lord, let me by guided in life by your great wisdom and teach me the knowledge of your powerful level of elevation in Jesus name.

I break every curse of fruitless labour placed upon my life, in the name of Jesus.

I break every curse of untimely death against my destiny, against my purpose or my elevation, in the name of Jesus.

Lord, fortify me with your power in Jesus name!

Let the countermovement of the Holy Spirit frustrate every evil device against the elevation on my life, in the name of Jesus.

Father Lord give me the tongues of fire that I can decree and declare your words so that I can reach the place of elevation in Jesus name.

Lord, make my voice the voice of peace, deliverance, power, and solution in my isolation period in Jesus name.

Lord, give me divine direction that will propel me to greatness and a powerful level of elevation in Jesus name

Every power assigned, to use my family/job, etc to torment me in my elevation, be paralysed, in the name of Jesus.

Lord Jesus, give me an excellent spirit in my time of isolation to elevate to greatness in Jesus name.

O Lord make me the head and not the tail of those who laugh at me, reject me, look down on me, talk bad about me, gossip about me, envy me, who are jealous of me or tear me down during my time of isolation in Jesus name.

Thank God for answering these prayers.

Epilogue

When going through **isolation** it will cause you to get to a place of **elevation**. This will give you a sense of **visualisation** in order to have an **exaltation** where you will have to go through a period of **mediation.** God will give you the correct ways of **interpretation**, in order for you to give the right **communication** to other believers in the body of Christ and the correct **translation** even to those who are not saved so they can come to a place of knowing who God truly is and why he needs to be accepted as their Lord and saviour Jesus Christ.

Please know that you cannot be of any good to others if you are no good to yourself. You cannot pour onto anything or anyone if your cup is empty. Being isolated gives you time to refill your own cup. It will give you time to study, catch up on some rest, routinely work out, pray, plan, meditate, and much more. From the moment

God puts you in isolation, that is the moment you for you to realise that you are about to be elevated.

CELEATH TURNER

- ✓ Ms. Celeath Turner- is the author of CHRISTIAN & BURNING: Sexual desires yet keeping it holy as well as Christian & Burning Prayer Journal: 52 Week - Let Go & Let God- Scriptures- Devotional & Guided Prayer Journal For Single Women, Unmasking The Spirit of Envy & Jealously in The Body of Christ

- ✓ Who lives in the United Kingdom with her two children, Michaela and Shanlee. As a single mother, she took time out to care for her children in the UK, where family support was skeletal.

- ✓ She is also a Prophetess and an ordained Evangelist in King Jesus Pentecostal Fellowship, UK branch. The church has its head office in Jamaica, with its leader being Apostle Winston Baker.

- ✓ She is a speaker and a preacher. Her mandate is to encourage Christians to further their walk with God, thus saving souls.

- ✓ Prophetess Evangelist Celeath holds a degree in Business & Humans Resource Management from the University of Wolverhampton, United Kingdom. She also holds an 132

- ✓ Associate Diploma in Christian Ministry from Middlesex University London.

- ✓ This woman of God is also the CEO & Founder of her cleaning company called Duplex Cleaning Solution.

- ✓ As this is her first book, she hopes that she will reach souls by blessing them and helping them overcome the situations they may find themselves in as relates to singledom.

Contact: Celeath@ hotmail.co.uk E mail
Duplexcleaningsolutionltd@ gmail.com

Mango Girl Group Ltd. Publishing is a service that helps you publishing your book no matter what stage it is at, contact us now at sales@themangogirl.com

Printed in Poland
by Amazon Fulfillment
Poland Sp. z o.o., Wrocław

60103752R00115